WWW.WithoutGodseries.com

A P3 Production Series

Special Thanks To:

"Jesus Christ"

Without God

A Novel by: *Loria Rogers*

First Edition

Published by P3 Productions

ISBN 978-0-578-16543-1

2015

Introduction

Without God is a story about a world of unbelieving people who feel as if God is just a made up myth created by man to bring fear to bad people. Day after day, more families, businesses and individuals began turning away from their belief in God, but rather to the belief of themselves, placing God in the same category as Santa Claus as we know him, a man made character.

Gods' name has become distorted and misused, by men and women of all ages, young boys and girls, and especially teenagers. The respect of the living God as we once knew him was no more. They made jokes about him, and laughed at him; they used his son's name Jesus Christ as a swearing word and cursed each other openly with it.

Each day the angels of God reported mankind's deeds and for several years, the reports remained the same. The people that God so loved and created, no longer felt as if they needed him anymore! It was the greatest heart break ever imagined. God, knowing the true desires of their hearts, had no other choice but to give them what their hearts truly desired, because he could never force a choice or decision on anyone.

Now that God has turned his back to us, the question remains, who then will be saved, without God!

Chapter 1

The Decision

The Archangels are meeting with GOD for their daily report. "My Lord, it is I, your servant Gabriel, with my report." God replies in a thundering voice "Speak my son; let your report be heard." Gabriel says, "Nothing has changed my Lord, for the humans speak the same language of hate as before."

The angel Michael adds, "My Lord, it is I your servant Michael, with my report." God answers "Speak my son; let your report be heard." "Nothing has changed my Lord; the humans speak the same as before."

Then the Angel Sinclair speaks, "My Lord, it is I your servant Sinclair, with my report." Again God says, "Speak my son, let your report be heard." The Angel Sinclair responds, "It remains the same my Lord, for nothing has changed."

Finally, the Angel Raphael speaks, "My Lord, it is I your servant Raphael, with my report." God answers "Speak my son; let your report be heard." The Angel Raphael says sadly, "Their hearts are yet cold my Lord, nothing has changed."

After hearing the angels' reports, God speaks, "After all I've done for them, how could their hearts turn so cold against me? I gave them life- I have kept them from hurt and disaster- I heal them when they are sick- regardless of their ways; I shielded them from death. I carried their burdens- I wake them up each morning- with the activity of their limbs- and whatever they asked in my son's name- I gave it to them. How could they turn from me? Is there at least one who still believes in me?"

The Angel Raphael asks, "My Lord, if I may speak? We have sent guardian angels throughout the nations, and their reports are that less than one percent has faith. If I may be so forward, I think you should give them what their cold and perverted heart's desire, and let them all know and see just who they really are without you!"

God responds, "For the sake of the percentage that has faith, I cannot turn away." The Angel Sinclair asks, "Lord if I may? The percentage in which you speak of is very small, for them let grace and mercy abide, but as an example for even the believers, let your absence be felt by all. Only then will man truly know the true desires of his own heart."

God asks, "Will all share the heart in which Sinclair speaks from?" The angles answered together, "**Indeed My Lord our hearts are shared alike.**" After hearing their response, God decides, "Then, so shall it be unto man! That on the 24th day of the twelfth month of the year 2017; My Grace and Mercy shall no longer abide among mankind; until the day man's heart truly and willingly returns to me! Therefore, let the abiding of my grace and mercy remains among my true believers, as my presence departs from all. I declare it by the heavens and by the earth, for I the Living God has spoken and so shall it be!"

Chapter 2

The cold hearts of man: The streets of Brooklyn, New York

August 2017

Two guys dive behind a parked car. "Godd*#*n Cuz, did you see that s**t, that nigga almost dropped us with dat f*&#in" drive- by, cuz who da f#*& wuz dat anyway? Let's go get that nigga man, he don't know who the f&%k he's f%$*in wit!"

"I feel you dog, let's go do this s#%t, let's show dat fool who da f%#@ he's f*#@in wit!"

They pulled out their guns and started running down a dark alley, to cut the driver off. As the car passes by, they both open fire, shooting the driver in the back of the head.

Atlanta, GA

A mother talks to her daughter, "Rhonda, I'm on my way to work, I won't be in till late, so don't forget to feed the dog, and I don't want nobody in my house while I'm gone- you hear me?" Rhonda answers facetiously, "Yes ma'am, I hear you loud and clear." I mean it Rhonda! Don't let me catch that boy in my house no more! "I said I heard you- god!" Mom squints her eyes at her daughter, and replies, "Um hum!"

Ten minutes after her mother leaves, Rhonda's cell phone rings. Her ringtone has a unique musical message, "I ain't down wit that s&#t." Lying across her bed, Rhonda answers, "What's up boo, where were you today, I didn't see you at school?" "What, for real, ooh you so bad." As she listens to the caller talking, she responds, "Whatever, that b*&%h" don't intimidate me." "That's a god*d# lie, I didn't tell that b*%$h nothing! The conversation continues, Naw, she gonna get f$#*ed up talking' that s*&t! Yeah- yeah whatever! Yeah, she left about 15 minutes ago; yeah she's working late tonight, again! She continues her conversation, "Naw, man she got me feeding this "god*&@n" dog, I don't even like that little mother*&%er! Alright boo, see you when you get here! Luv u too bye!"

Hollywood, California

A wealthy family's decision

Its 11:00am, a husband talks to his wife, while she's relaxing outside in the sun by their beautiful, ocean view pool. The husband, Tyler, is getting ready for work. He enters the patio area fixing his tie, "Susan honey, I might be a little late tonight, the stocks are up and it's looking real good for us." He says.

"Tyler, you're not still betting on those stupid horse races are you?" she responds sarcastically. "Susan, I said STOCK, not GAMBLING!" "Your stock normally ends in gambling dear." She responds. "Are you going to start this s*&% again, I made one bet- one time, and you will never let me forget it!" She snaps. "Yes, I'm going to start that s%#t again, that "one" time" nearly cost us a fortune!" She reminds him. "Cost "us" a fortune or "you" a fortune? Anyway, what the hell, are you so worried about, your "daddy" isn't going to let his little girl want for anything!" Tyler replies.

Sipping on a martini while standing in the shallow part of the pool, Susan says, "My daddy doesn't have anything to do with your gambling. His fortune is merely a blessing of God and knowledge!" Surprised, Tyler responds, "GOD? Woman, the only God you know is that bottle, and the only God your daddy knows- is the God of rip off!"

"Well, my daddy's God never seemed to be of any concern of yours before; as long as you had it to spend on those d&%m horses!" she mentions. Turning to leave the patio with a smirk on his face, he says, "Your daddy invented the horse tracks." Susan angrily, throws her martini glass at him as he leaves and yells, "liar! My daddy never gambled a day in his life!"

Seattle, Washington

A Baptist church in progress

Pastor Charles is in the pulpit preaching, "Oh lift your hands to God and worship him in this place, for he is truly worthy of the praise. Is there anyone in the house of God tonight that desires prayer, just come on down and meet me at the altar."

A middle-aged woman in her late 30's, walks to the altar with a short skirt and low cut blouse. Appearing to be concerned, Pastor says, "Sweet child of God, what would you like God to do for you tonight?" The woman leans over to whisper her prayer requests in the Pastors' ear, "Well Reverend, she whispers softly, "I really want you to touch me and ease my lonely pain."

Placing his hand on her shoulder as if to pray for her; and his other hand on her chest between her breasts he pulls her closer and whispers, "I can feel your pain, and I would love to ease your pain after service, in my office." Throwing her hands up as though she's praising God, Yes! Yes! I receive it, I receive it! She walks back to her seat with her hands to her face as if she was crying.

New Hope, Virginia

A Christian family gathers around the table for dinner. Grandmother seated at the table prays, "Thank, you Lord for this meal that's prepared for us this day, bless it and sanctify it for the body, and bless the ones who prepared it, we thank you Lord and give you the glory for all things in Jesus mighty name we pray. Amen." The family responds, "Amen!"

Two months later, October 31 Halloween

For religious reasons, some people don't celebrate man-made holidays, although it was ok for them to worship idols. Some do not believe in Jesus as the Christ, others had problems with the Trinity. Those who do believe in man-made holidays decorate their towns and homes; dress their children up as demons and witches, who roam the streets at night going from house to house gathering candy.

Many Christian groups would host Halloween Contests at their churches, giving prizes for the best-looking angel or cartoon characters. Everybody had their own reasons for doing what they did and how they did it.

During the Month of November, the holidays of Thanksgiving, are no longer about families gathering together acknowledging thanks to God. Instead, it became a money making day for businesses and restaurants. Each year, more people become depressed, because of the lack of money or absent family members, due to broken homes.

Buffet restaurants look forward to making major profits from families of two, three, four and sometimes eight members, who no longer have the desire to cook together. Thanksgiving as they knew it, was just another holiday habit.

Only a few Thanksgiving decorations are displayed, instead, businesses stock their shelves with Christmas items, toys and gifts, as if Thanksgiving never existed. The one holiday that man chose to give thanks to God, was no longer a holiday of thanks, but for profit.

December 1, 2017

23 days remaining of God's Grace and Mercy

Businesses prosper as the habit of Christmas spreads across the world, for those who believe it. Many people utilize every resource they have- bank withdrawals- saving bond- checking accounts- life savings- stocks- bonds- credit cards and more- for the purchasing of Christmas gifts.

On this day, families will come together, celebrating around a decorated tree with flashing lights; giving thanks to one another for gifts they receive from beneath a tree. Where did the purpose go?

What happened to the true meaning of Christmas? They adopted only one part of the Christmas story, the gifts given to baby Jesus at his birth. The true question is, what about baby Jesus?

December 15, 2017

The airlines are booked in advance for the early arrival of family members. Rental cars are reserved- bus tickets purchased- some arrive by train and others even by boat. It doesn't matter how they get there, they just get there any way they can. Through all of the chaos, not even one of them felt the need to offer unto God, a prayer of protection as they travel. The assumption of natural safety has undoubtedly poisoned their belief.

December 20, 2017

4 days remaining of God's Grace and Mercy

Blessed are those who arrive safely in these last days of Grace and Mercy. For no one knows the wrath of God, during these Godless times of the mere turn of his face. However, the expectancy of pleasurable visits and safe arrivals may not be achievable if we were to get what we truly deserve, rather than the

Grace that kept us from it. Imagine the world in which you live, solely based upon your own actions.

December 23, 2017

The Spoken word of God

The Archangels of God are standing beside him as he declares his wrath unto man. "As I have declared by the heavens and by the earth, so shall it be, at the 24th hour of the 24th day of year 2017, my Grace and Mercy shall no more abide among mankind, until the day in which their hearts shall willingly turn back to me!" The Archangels respond, "So shall it be upon the earth."

Grocery stores and supermarkets are running out of stock due to the Christmas Eve rush. Last minute, Christmas shoppers trying to buy gifts are overcrowding the stores.

Brooklyn, New York

Tyrone and Mike, the two men involved in the drive-by shooting back in August; are chilling on the front porch of Tyrone's mother's house. Tyrone is laid back in a chair, drinking a bottle of whiskey. Mike asks, "What time is it man?"

"About- 7:30 why?" Mike responds. "No reason cuz, just seeing what's up." Mike asks, "Yo T, so what you and your mom's got up for Christmas, she cooking?" Tyrone responds, "Cuz, my mom ain't cooked in so long, I forgot what her cooking taste like. Sh%t man, we don't celebrate that Christmas buls#%t no mo! Ever since she hooked up wit dat fool that got her hooked on that sh#t, all she wanna do is get high and f%#k!"

Mike replies, "What!" You mean to tell me she still messin wit dat fool?" Angrily Tyrone replies, "Yeah cuz, I don't know what she see in that nigga man, he ain't even got no job! I can't stand that nigga man!"

Tyrone Changing the subject, "So what's up wit you cuz, what you got going on?" "My boy Kilo is DJ'ing at Club Mac tonight, I was gonna stop by and check 'em out. Why you wanna hang?" Mike asks.

"Naw man, for some strange reason, I got a bad feeling about tonight, I just don't know what it is cuz!" Tyrone said. "What kind of bad feeling' you got man?" Tyrone explains, "I don't know cuz, ever since we hit that nigga in the alley that night, sh&t just don't feel right. I don't know- maybe I'm just tripin cuz- f*&% it, let's hit da club tonight man." Concerned, Mike asks, "You sure bout dat man, I mean I don't want you trippin' tonight." "Naw cuz, I'm straight- I got this cuz- I got dis." Tyrone relies.

Atlanta, GA

Rhonda's in her mother's house with her boyfriend Terry, even though her mother forbids him to be there. "Hold up boo, where's your condom?" "Girl, I don't need no condom, I'm straight!" Terry replies. "What chu mean- "you straight", I ain't trying' to have no baby Terry!" Rhonda says sounding agitated. "Baby," ain't nobody want no God&%$ baby! That's the least of your worries!"

"I just wanna feel you girl; I know when to pull up. You act like it's our first time without a condom- girl stop trippin!"

"I'm not trippin' Terry- you know if you keep playing wit fire you gonna get burnt!" Terry gets her straight, "Girl," you already burnt! Now bring your sexy a#s over here and let me get up in it." Reluctantly she agrees, "O-k Terry, but you better pull up dis time!" He reassures her, "Yeah whatever, you know I got you girl!"

Hollywood, California

Tyler working late with his secretary

"Mr. Chapman" secretary Sherri says. "Please, Sherri, call me Tyler." Secretary Sherri responds, "Ok then, "Tyler," if you need to go I can finish here, I know how busy you are." "Sherri, what would I do without you?" Tyler says, she replies, "Well, hopefully you will never have to find out." He laughs, "You're certainly right about that; I guess I'll see you in the morning then Sherri, goodnight." Secretary Sherri replies cordially, "Yes in the morning, goodnight to you to sir, I mean "Tyler."

Walking to his car, he is approached by his wife's father, Gary Chandler in the parking lot. "Tyler, wait a minute, I want to talk to you", Gary asks. Tyler stops before getting into his car. Tyler responds, "Oh, hi, what's up Mr. Chandler?

"Please, call me Gary. I've been trying to catch up with you concerning a project that may be of interest to you." He says. Curiously Tyler asks "What sort of project are we talking about?" Gary responds, "One that requires more of a private atmosphere. What'll you say we meet for lunch tomorrow- it's on me, then we can talk better." "Sure, that's fine, is one o'clock good for you?" Gary asks, "One o'clock will be fine, oh, and by the way, try not to mention our little meeting to Susan; she tends to worry about the wrong things if you know what I mean."

Tyler nods his head, "huh- do I, she is her father's child; don't worry Gary, your secret is safe with me." "Good, then tomorrow it is. Goodnight Tyler." Tyler agrees, "Yeah, you too Gary."

Seattle, Washington

Pastor Charles, of the Baptist Church is home with his family. His wife Karen reminds him, "Charles, you forgot to get the cranberry sauce for our Christmas dinner." "You know what, I sure did, I guess- his cell phone rings interrupting him, -"hold on honey, let me see who this is calling me on the evening before Christmas Eve." He looks at the number, "Oh this is Brother Barnes, I guess he wants to know what's for dinner." He laughs. "I'll talk to him on my way to get your cranberry sauce." He says as he holds the cell phone down.

"Ok honey- and could you pick up some celery as well- thank you- love you honey." "Will do, love you too baby. Pastor Charles replies,

Getting in his car, Pastor Charles angrily answers the phone, "What the Hell are you doing calling me when I'm with my family?"

The caller responds, "Well Charles- that's not the only family you have you know; we're about to start our own family in May." Pastor Charles says sternly, "I told you that I would take care of that, I already have a family! I can't tell my wife that I have another baby on the way in five more months!"

"Take care of what, Charles? I am not about to give up our baby, to save your precious wife from knowing about our child; you should've thought about that before your decided to answer my prayers in your office that night!" The woman says.

He arrives at the store.

"Look Sarah! I got to go, I'll talk with you later, I can't talk right now!" He says quickly. "Later," When Charles? How much longer do I have to wait for you to leave her and be with your new family; who loves you and knows how to treat a man like you?" Sarah asks. "What are you talking about?

Sarah I'm not about to leave my family for your bastard child!" He said angrily, "Bastard child! Charles- it's your child! How could it be a bastard child? My child has a father, and he will be a part of our lives, one way or another!" Sarah yells as she hangs up the phone. "Sarah! – Sarah! That God*da%n woman is going to make me-huh!" He walks in the grocery store.

There was a homeless man who walked the streets of Los Angeles every night trying to tell everyone who passed by, about the future that's to come, but everyone just ignores him in their passing. It was another one of God's Angels trying to reach the people before it was too late.

Speaking to anyone who'll listen, the homeless man says, "Repent for the wrath of God is at hand! Repent I say to you, listen to the words of the Lord. How merciful has he been to you all? His Grace kept you safe from disaster. Why have you hardened your hearts to the warnings of the master? Repent I tell you! Repent for the wrath of God is at hand! Who will be able to stand in your hour of need without the Mercies and Grace of our living God? Repent, I tell you, repent!"

The city clock sounds off indicating the 24th hour, that renders man Grace and merciless.

The homeless man, who has for the past several months, walked the streets of LA, disappears into thin air and no one even noticed.

Chapter 3

Hell on Earth

Being that the mindset of the people wasn't erased, no one would truly know of the absence of Grace and Mercy until adversity struck. Only then would they begin to feel the absence of peace. There is only God who is good, and Satan who is evil. A world without God faces the pure evil within, which had been previously shielded by Grace and Mercy.

For some of the people, the warm feeling of excitement and anticipation fill their hearts while they await the arrival of their relatives; only to discover great sorrows of their crash landings. For others, the busy holiday roads never sleep, even when the lengthy driving hours of fatigue causes many cars to drift into oncoming traffic.

Holidays would not be much of a celebration, without our intoxicated motorists; who forced an entire family into an oncoming lane of convoys, causing the death of over 180 holiday travelers heading home.

Without God who then will save us from disaster?

As of the 24th hour of the 24th day of 2017, over 350,000 lives were lost before the clock struck 1:00am. Inasmuch, heaven mourns for the lost souls.

What started out as holiday cheer turns out to be a holiday no one would ever forget. The next morning, Christmas Day, all of the fatalities that took place on Christmas Eve, were being broadcast on TV news channels everywhere.

Families everywhere mourned for the loss of their loved ones. Christmas Day without God was not to be a celebrated day.

Because that was the day Christ, his Son was born, and no man goes to the father except through the Son. For that reason, if man couldn't honor the Son of God's day of birth, then neither would God honor their lives.

The absence of Grace and Mercy began to shine very bright on man's inner being; making clear the true desires of their hearts and how far down man would go, without the boundaries of the fear of God.

Atlanta, Georgia

Rhonda is at the mall, one week after Christmas on New Year's Eve; looking around a skinny jean store. One of her enemies, Kelli, the most popular girl at school, was there too. Rhonda has gained weight since the holiday break from school. "Excuse me ma'am, how much are these jeans?" She asks. "Good choice sweetie, we just got those jeans in today, they're a special cut. Those are $35, it's a great deal!" The sales lady says trying to make a sale.

Leery of the price Rhonda replies, "Well, yeah, but $35 for just one pair of jeans, wow!" "You know, it really is a good deal" The sales lady persist.

Turning around, Rhonda notices Kelli and tries to be friendly even though she doesn't like her. "Oh, what's up Kelli?" "Not much, just shopping. What about you?' Kelli responds. Rhonda rolls her eyes as if to say duh! "Uh- shopping!" Kelli sarcastically says, "Well- don't you think you're in the wrong store, I mean the sign clearly says SKINNY jeans. And from the looks of it, there's nothing skinny about you anymore!" Turning back around, ignoring her statement, "Whatever Kelli, -uh- ma'am do you have this in any other color?" "Oh yeah, I forgot, black is said to make one appear thinner", Kelli instigates.

Now Rhonda is aggravated. She turns back around and snaps, "What the f*#k is your problem Kelli! You can't find nobody else to harass today, so you gotta f*#@ with me? Bi*&h you really need to back the hell up off me, before I f%@k you up!"

Smiling deviously, Kelli softly says, "TEMPER! TEMPER! Now why would you want to f%#k me up? I mean I do understand misery loves company; but d#*n girl, that's really cruel and very selfish of you, to wanna f%&* a sista up because a nigga f*&%ed you up!" Looking confused Rhonda asks, "What the f#@* are you talking about?" "What!" You mean to tell me that you don't know? Everybody in town knows!" Kelli says still smiling deviously, "Know what b#@*&," Rhonda asks angrily. Kelli responds, "Wait", you are kickin' it wit Terry right?" Rhonda replies, "Yeah! So what's your f@#$%n point?" "Wow! You really don't know do you" Kelli lingers?"

"KNOW WHAT!" Rhonda yells. "Girl! Terry is boiling! Rhonda's confused, "What the hell do boiling mean?" "He's hot bi&@h- boiling hot!" Now looking really confused, Rhonda asks, Hot as in what, "sexy?"

"HELL NAW!" Bi*#h! "Hot as in "Hot!" F*&%ed up- Done for- Grave yard done! All I gotta say is that you really need to get yourself checked out; he might of f#@*&d you up with a two for one! I mean, it doesn't take a rocket scientist to realize how big you got. Ha,

ANYway- have a good one!" Kelli smiles as she walks out the store with her shopping bags.

Shocked, Rhonda slowly lowers the jeans back on the table staring into space wondering. "Oh My God Terry! What have you done to me?"

Brooklyn, New York

Tyrone and Mike are at a local bar shooting pool and drinking. "Come on cuz, it ain't like dat is it? You kicking a nigga's a%s boy!" Tyrone says jokingly. "What nigga, I told you no mercy!" Mike replies, He leans across the table to make a shot, when a fair skinned girl with long black hair from across the room, wearing short- shorts- a tank top - red lipstick and 5-inch stiletto heels- walks up behind him and pushes her body against him, causing him to miss his shot.

"WHAT THE" as he turns around fast, changing his attitude once he sees her. In a soft voice, she says, "Oh- I'm sorry- did I do that? My bad, I guess I lost my balance and kind of fell into you." "DAAAAAAMN!" "Tyrone says. Mike jumps in, "Girl, you can fall into me ANY time!" Tyrone asks, "What's your name ma?" "Candy", she replies softly. "I can see dat!" Tyrone says looking her up and down.

Mike jumps in again, "For real, for real!" Tyrone asks, "Where your man at? I know you got one somewhere!" Speaking in a soft voice, Candy replies "Why I gotta have a man? Why can't it just be me?" Mike says, "You right! Cause if you were my girl, I da%n sho won't let you out lookin like dat!"

Candy smiles, "Is there something wrong with the way I look?" She slowly slides her fingers through her hair. "HELL NO!" Tyrone exclaims. "Not from where I'm standing!" says Mike. Tyrone asks again, "For real though, where yo man at?" Candy explains, "Well, if you really must know, he was taken from me about 5 months ago. It was tragic and it took me about that long to get out again. I'm just a firm believer- that- what goes around- really does come back around. Um- but that's just me." Tyrone wants to know more, "Wow" Ma, sorry to hear that- you said tragic, so what happened?"

"I'm not really sure, from what I was told, he was on his way home, when a couple of stray bullets got him in the back of the head. The crazy thing about it- was that he didn't die right away; he was able to say a few things before he died. I was told that he said he truly loves me. Then he mentioned some guy's name and then he died. My world- was over- I loved him so very much." She said as her eyes begin to water.

"We were planning to get married and have some kids, I had just"- she pauses as a tear falls down her face. "I had just left the doctor earlier that day. I called him to tell him that he was going to be a father. He was so happy, that he drove down the street shooting his gun in the air.

He told me that he loved me and that he was on his way home to show me just how much. Needless to say, he never made it. I'm sorry," as she pushes a tear slowing to the side of her face regaining composure. "I really thought I was over it, but I guess I'm not." Both Mike and Tyrone look serious after hearing her sad story, "da%n girl, dat's some heavy sh%t!" Mike says sadly. "Wow ma! I don't know what to say." Tyrone says awkwardly.

Switching the subject, Candy says, "Well, I'm kind of hungry, you boys wanna get something to eat?" Mike asks, "Where you wanna go? "I don't know"- She said looking around, "Somewhere quiet and not as many people."

"There's a spot down the way, not far from here dat has a nice quiet atmosphere. We can go there." Suggested Tyrone, "Yeah, yeah, I know dat spot, me and my boys used to chill there." Mike agrees.

"Cool! Let's bounce." Tyrone says taking Candy by the waist. "Ok, let me go tell my girls I'm out."

Curious, Mike says, "Your girls! Are they as hot as you?" Candy responds, "Um- have you ever heard of a girl- hanging with girls- who's less than she is?" Mike smiles, "So then what's up? The more the merrier." "Well- let me see if they wanta cut out too." Candy walks back across the room. Tyrone tells her, "Yeah, you do dat- just make sure you come back."

Mike turns to look at Tyrone, "Man, how you gonna holla at ole girl, when she pushed up on me first? "Cuz, you were so trapped by her beauty, dat you lost your ability to speak and you know what da say, a closed mouth don't get fed!" Tyrone smiles, Mike laughs as he tosses the pool stick across the table, "Man you stupid!" They both start laughing.

Candy and three of her girlfriends walk back across the room towards Mike and Tyrone. Candy introduces her friends, "Sonja- Dajah- Courtney- this is Mike and Tyrone. Mike, Tyrone, this is Sonja- Dajah- and Courtney." Tyrone flirts, "I should've known dat candy only hang with sugar!" Mike agrees, "And how sweet it is!"

"So ladies, you ready to roll?" Asks Tyrone; Candy answers for them; "We'll follow you."

Arriving at the restaurant, the guys help the girls out of their car. As they enter the building, they notice a small dance floor on the right side of the room and a very elegant table setting on the other. The restaurant was a small, but very romantic place.

They sit together in an oval booth. Tyrone sits next to Candy on the end and Dajah sits on the other side of Candy, Courtney sits beside Dajah, and Mike sits in between Courtney and Sonja. Mike tells everyone, "They made some changes since the last time I kicked it here. That dance floor wasn't there and the tables were positioned different." Tyrone looking around agrees, "Yeah you right- it was- looks good though."

The waiter came over to their table to get their drink and food orders. After placing their orders; they all sat around talking and chilling, until Candy's favorite slow song starts to play over the speakers. "Oh sh#t, that's my jam!" She says, as she starts to groove to the music in her seat. "So what's up ma, you wanna dance?" Asks Tyrone, Candy slowly runs her fingers through her hair, behind her ear, "Sure, why not?"

Tyrone takes Candy by the hand and leads her to the dance floor. Swaying slowly to the music, Candy moves closer to Tyrone. He places his hands around her waist and gently pulls her body to his. Looking her in the eyes, he softly says, "You are sooo beautiful.

I really hate what happened to you. You deserve so much more than that. I can see how somebody can love you so much, you're just so sweet. I could love you forever." With teary eyes, she replies, "I don't think I could ever love again. I don't even know what to do now that he's gone. I don't even know- who I am anymore. My outer shell may be beautiful- but I feel so ugly inside." She looks down as her tears fall.

"Ma, what happened to yo man, should not affect who you are. Cause to me, you're beautiful on the outside and the inside. I know you get lonely sometimes, but you ain't got to be alone. I'll be here for you; and I'm not asking you to love me, I'm asking you to let me love on you, and not sexually. I just want to be that shoulder that you cry on, and dat friend that can make you laugh. I want you to smile again. I got you ma, I got you." He reassures her. Softly pushing her tears away with his finger, she lifts her head to look into his eyes and he gently kisses her.

Hollywood, California

Tyler is working in his office. Secretary Sherri calls him on his speaker phone, "Mr. Chapman, you have a call on line one. It's your father in-law Mr. Gary Chandler." "Thank you Sherri, you can put him through." He says frowning his face in discuss. "Tyler my boy, are we still on for lunch today?" Gary asks.

"Yeah- sure, it's looking pretty good on this end. Where did you want to meet?" Gary responds, "Let's meet at Randle's Steak House, on the South side of town." "Why so far?" Tyler asks, "There's somebody I want you to meet, he owns that restaurant, "Gary explains. "Alright- whatever, I'll be there within the hour" Tyler says tired of hearing his voice.

"What time is it now Gary looks at his clock, 12:20?- So about, say 1:20", Gary asks? Tyler agrees, "Yeah, something like that!" "Ok, see you then." Tyler hangs up the phone. He's never been a big fan of Susan's father. He thinks he's a spineless manipulator, who uses any and every one to get what he wants. For this reason he handles Gary in a cautious manner.

1:54pm. On the Southside of town, Tyler pulls up at the restaurant. Entering the building he could see Gary at the bar talking to another man. He walks over to the bar. "Well, well, look who decided to show up" Gary smiles. "Yeah, well, I had to handle some last minute stuff. So what's up?" asks Tyler.

"Tyler, he says with a big smile, "I want you to meet a very close friend of mine. I told him all about you." Tyler knows there must be a catch. "Really," That can't be good!" Gary continues, "Randle, this is my son in-law Tyler, a very bright and wise young man." Tyler, thinks to himself, oh great- what is this sleaze ball cooking up now? Randle is a black man, who owns the steak house on the Southside of California. Gary and Randle have been friends since they were in Vietnam.

Tyler tries to rush the conversation along, "So Gary, what is this all about? What kind of meeting is this supposed to be, and why is it so important for me to meet this person?" Gary tries to slightly change the subject, "Why don't we all just sit down and enjoy a wonderful lunch." Randle asks, "Tyler, so what exactly is it that you do?" Tyler responds, "Well, to my understanding, Gary has already supplied you with my information! So tell me, what exactly is it that "YOU" do?"

Randle laughs, "Gary, you were right about your son-in-law. He's quite the fire ball. That could be just the thing I'm looking for." Tyler asks "Um, looking for as in what?" Turning to look at Gary Randle frowns. "Gary, "I see you haven't discussed any of this with him yet, have you?" Gary explains, "No, not yet, I thought it would be better if we all sat down together, for a better understanding."

Randle leans back in his chair with his arms crossed and frowns, "better understanding about what, you've lost all of your money and now you need to rebuild, it's as simple as that!" He says bluntly.

Tyler stands up in front of his chair and raises his voice, "YOU HAVE GOT TO BE JOKING. "Hah" a short laugh, you mean to tell me that you lost all of your crooked money and you want me to help you restore it? You're a piece of work! I underestimated you Gary, you're human after all! I "NEVER" thought I'd see the day when "Gary Chandler" would grovel at my feet! "I am SO going to enjoy this!" Gary is too ashamed to speak.

Sitting back down, Tyler leans back in his chair with his arms folded behind his head smiling big, "So- tell me Mister- "Randle"- is it? How can I be of assistance to you?" Randle responds, "Well, "Tyler" Gary tells me about your eye for the horse tracks and we just placed three thoroughbred winners out there. With the right attention, it could be quite profitable for all of us."

Trying to understand the situation "So let me get this straight, you want me to advertise your illegal horses through my company- am I clear on that?" "What makes you think they're illegal?" Randle replies; "Ok- well- let's see- Tyler leans back again with his hand on his chin as if to be thinking.

"Out of all of my years of running the tracks, the one thing I know for sure, is that each and every horse has to have papers- important papers- State papers- in which your horses do not! BECAUSE, if in fact they did have them; we would not be having this conversation slash meeting, with one of the biggest crooks in California- My dear ole step-father- who may I add, does not want his dear ole daughter to know about! So- you tell me Mr. Randle- legal or illegal?"

New Hope, Virginia - New Year's Day

Grandma Ames and her daughter are getting ready for Sunday morning service. Grandma is watching the news while getting dressed. "Brenda! Brenda- come in here and look at this here news, the world done gone crazy!" She says in disbelief. "Coming mama, Brenda runs in the room with her. What happened?" "Look a here, some young crazy white boy done shot and killed nine people in a church in North Carolina- and in Tennessee somewhere another one dun shot and killed some cops. Lord Jesus- all them people done gone crazy, people killing each other, folks robbing and stealing from each other, Lord what in the world is going on", Grandma Ames asks?

"Listen at that!" Staring intensely at the TV screen.; "Oh my God, look at that, folks burning up churches and shooting up movie theaters: and- Oh my God- preachers done walked away from their own churches.

Lord Jesus, what kind of mess is that?" She asks shaking her head in unbelief. "Look mama, the churches are almost empty, what in the world is going on mama, it's almost like they all gave up on God or something" says Brenda.

"Either that or God done gave up on them!" "You mean God can give up on you mama?" "Baby, God can do whatever he wants to do, he's God! People don't realize how much God does for them. It's just not about what people can do to others- they don't realize what they're doing to themselves! Baby, God is love-God is peace- God is joy in the midst of sorrow.

God brings families together, he's such a loving God that he places his arms of protection around those of us who know he's

God- and willingly love and obey his word!"
She continues,

"Without God baby, this world would be a mess; people already don't have the fear no mo! Look how they dun give rights to abominations against God! The world dun gone away from the truth in his word! But a world without God- means the end of peace-joy-love-forgiveness-understanding-deliverance- healing- and so much more- baby God is our everythang!

This world will be in such a mess, that they wouldn't need to wonder who's gona destroy them; cause without God, they'll be in such a grieving state of mind - that they'll destroy themselves. Without God baby, who then- can be saved?" Come on baby; let's get ready to go on to church."

Seattle, Washington - New Year's Day

Monday evening Pastor Charles is in the sanctuary alone praying.

"Lord Jesus, I know you said that you will be with me, and I know I have not been the best that I could be. I can't say that I truly believe everything I preach about, and I'm not even sure you said anything the Bible said you did; in fact I don't even know why or what I'm even doing here at all today. I just thought I'd try just one more time before I walked away from my belief in you. If you truly exist, I'm so sorry, but if you don't, then I'm just a da&n fool here talking to myself. Either way, I can't do this anymore, good bye!" Pastor Charles says dejectedly.

Getting up off his knees, Sarah walks in the door just as he's done with his prayer. Turning around he could see a dark shadow around her. "I thought I'd find you in here." Sarah says, curiously, Pastor Charles stares at the shadow around her, "What in the hell? What is that?"

Sarah looking in his eyes, "What is what? What are you looking at, it's me sugar, I came to see you in the very place I knew you'd be." Pastor Charles responds, "How did you know that I would be here, I never told anybody where I was going?" Sarah smiles deviously, "I told you- we were meant to be together;   I can feel you wherever you go. It's almost like- like I'm apart of you, and you are a part of Me."

He never noticed her slowly floating closer to him, "You can't run from it Charles, you know you want it, you know you need it, and I- I got to have it!" She pulls his body to hers and kisses him passionately in the sanctuary. Unable to control himself, he puts his hands around her waist and slides them up her blouse. She slides her hands down his body quickly undoing his belt. Slowly, they ease to the floor at the altar, having passionate sex.

Moaning, Sarah says, "Oh Charles, I need you so much. We can be together forever now, come with me Charles- come with us- join us! I love you!" Charles is unable to speak, He in his heart, wants so badly to push her off of him, but because he rejected God, he now has no power to fight. The dark cloud around her body begins to circle the ceiling of the church, those without God's Grace and Mercy were compelled to go into the church.

They came from everywhere, men and men, women and women, men and women, even homeless people enter the church. Seeing the Pastor and Sarah in the passionate act of sex, turns the Church into one big orgy, with everyone having sex with each other. Pastor Charles seeing the people in this horrible state tries to get up, but he's held to the floor by the evil spirits surrounding Sarah, and he can't stop having sex.

Tears roll down his face as he sees the people entering the building; realizing that there's nothing he can do to stop it, he shuts his eyes saying: "My God, My God- What have I done!" Men and men, women and women, men and women, everyone was having uncontrolled sex in the sanctuary. It was a sanctuary that no longer belonged to God, but to hell in the flesh.

Pastor Charles's wife, Karen is on her way home from the supermarket which is in the direction of the church. Driving by the church she sees cars parked in every direction in front of the church, some cars even have the engines still running. Pulling over to see what's going on, she walks up the sidewalk towards the door. Approaching the door, a dark cloud fills the doorway and a powerful force throws her back. She falls to the ground. She smells a foul odor coming from the church, like nothing she'd ever smelled before. It was almost like the smell of burning brimstones.

With tears running down her face, she falls to her knees with her face to the ground and begins to talk to God. "My God, My God, turn not your face from me at this hour, for I your servant can clearly recognize the work of the enemy's curse upon this house. I pray that my husband is not within, but if he is, then he is no longer my husband anyway. Although I can't feel you, I do know you're real in my heart. I do believe that what I am about to do

- is your will- for this is no longer the house of God, but of Satan in the flesh!" She cries.

Her eyes were so full of tears, she could barely see. She goes to the storage house behind the church and grabs the gas can with gasoline used for the lawnmower, and the candle lighters used for the altar worship torches.

She starts from the back of the church pouring gasoline against the side of the building, until the side of each wall is laced with gasoline. Falling to her knees she takes one last look at what used to be their family church, and says to God, "Forgive me Father, if I am wrong, but on this day, I return Hell....back to Hell!"

Rising from her knees she strikes the lighter and tosses it onto a trail of gasoline that lead to the building and within minutes the church goes up in flames. Charles's wife Karen leaves the church and drives home barely able to see the road. Pulling in the driveway, she could hear the fire trucks heading towards the church.

Her daughter Rachael, 17 and her son Samuel, 19 are on their way out, when they hear their mother drive up. They go out to meet her in the driveway. Seeing her eyes full of tears, they rush to comfort her. Daughter Rachael asks, "What is it mother, what's wrong, is it daddy?"

Unable to speak through the tears, she just shakes her head in shock.

Her son Samuel says "Come in the house and sit down mama, come on, I got you, whatever it is, I know God will fix it." Helping their mother into the house, Samuel sits on the couch with his arms around his mother, comforting her as she weeps.

Chapter 4

Will they Surrender All?

Man's insight of himself caused more harm than physical weapons. The lack of peace- love- joy- and happiness-rendered them all too long suffering, Destroying themselves with their own hearts desires. A fate that caters to the hands of grief- hurt- sorrow- and greed, until death do they part! Unless God's Grace and Mercy returns to mankind, all of whom and what they are... will be lost.

Atlanta, GA

The New Year 2018 -January 2nd

Rhonda is sleeping in late, Rhonda's mother Tammy is on her phone talking to her girlfriend, enjoying her day off. "Yeah girl, I saw it on the news last night that was so sad, a church full of people just burned to the ground- hum? What did you say- um- um- no- it was in Washington State somewhere. I don't know, they didn't say what caused the fire. I know that's right girl, yeah girl, I'm thinking about going out tonight, but I don't know yet- ok- just let me know what you're going to do- ok bye."

"RHONDA! RHONDA!!! ARE YOU UP?" Walking upstairs to her room she opens Rhonda's door. "Rhonda- girl, do know what time it is, why are you sleeping so much lately?" She asks.

With her head under the covers, she says, "Mom, leave me alone, I'm just tired gosh!" Her mother responds, "Tired from what, you ain't got no job, how in the world can you be so tired?" Pulling the covers from her head, she forgets who she's talking too. "Why I gotta have a job to be tired ma, can't I just be tired of all the bull- Rhonda cuts her word short, remembering who she's talking to.

"I know you weren't going to say what I thought you were going to say, girl you done lost your mind! Get your butt out of that bed and get this room cleaned up! Since you got so much time on your hands, take your dirty clothes down stairs to the laundry room and wash that mess!" Her mother scolds! "Yes ma'am, I'm getting up!"

Tammy closes the door and walk back down the stairs. Rhonda lays there for about five more minutes and then slowly gets up and walks to the bathroom. Looking in the mirror at herself, she remembers everything Kelli had said to her in the mall.

Wishing it was all a bad dream, she breaks down crying hysterically, her mother hears her loud cries, rushes back up the stairs. Seeing her daughter in the floor crying uncontrollably, she knows something is seriously wrong, she falls to her knees beside her and pulls her daughter into her arms comforting her. Not understanding her daughter's pain she cry's with her, while trying to get her daughter to talk.

"Rhonda! Baby what's wrong, talk to me baby, tell me what's wrong!" She pleads. Holding her daughters head to her chest, baby, mama can't help you if I don't know what's wrong!" Unable to speak through her tears, she lays helplessly in her mother's arms crying. "Baby, PLEASE, talk to me, what's wrong with you, did somebody hurt you? What is it baby-what's wrong, tell me what's wrong!"

Calming down, holding her daughter's face in her hands, she continues, "Baby look at me-what is going on? This is not like you to act like this, so I know something is wrong. What can I do to help baby? Just tell me how I can make this better! I want to help you, but I just don't know how. You gotta talk to me baby-you gotta tell me what's wrong!" her mother pleads.

As she calms down, Rhonda looks in her mother's eyes and begins to talk, with her eyes full of tears, "Mama, I messed up! ... I messed up real bad!" Tammy looking very concerned, asks, "You messed up how baby? What did you do?"

Rhonda replies, "This time I really messed up. I don't know what to do, I just don't know!" She starts to cry again. "Baby what are you talking about, you messed up how? What happened- what did you do Rhonda? What did you do?" Her mother begs. "Momma, I'm so sorry for not listening to you, I should've listened- but now- it's too late mama- It's too late- I think Terry - gave me the virus -the AIDS virus mama- the AIDS virus!

She falls into her mother's arms crying. In a state of shock, her mother just sits there

44

speechless, holding her with her eyes full of tears.

Brooklyn, New York

Tyrone and Candy have been spending a lot of time together and she is beginning to trust him more and more. Saturday morning Tyrone spent a night at Candy's house but they did not get sexually intimate. Candy is up early making breakfast for Tyrone. Tyrone enters the kitchen in his pajama pants with no shirt. "She's beautiful and she cooks." He says kissing her on the back of her neck. Smiling, she turns around to kiss him. "Thank you, not just for the compliment, but also for a wonderful night that made me feel so safe and loved." She smiles.

Holding her waist, looking into her eyes, he reassures her. "I told you ma, I got you, and I ain't gonna let you go." He leans into her and kisses her passionately. Smelling her eggs about to burn, she gently pulls away from him. "Oh no" "My eggs" She says. "It's all good, we'll just have some Cajun eggs' He responds jokingly. "Whatever! You're so silly"

They both sit down to breakfast indulging into a deep conversation. "Don't worry ma, your eggs are fine, I told you it's all good.' "Well thank you, even though I know you don't mean it." She smiles. "Naw ma, for real, it's all good." Still smiling;" If you say so." Tyrone changes the subject. "You know ma, I've been thinking bout what you said about cho man."

"You said that you called him about being a father, I had been meaning to ask you about the baby; what happened to it?" Staring down at her plate, she responds, "I lost it. I- stressed out so much about losing Tony; that I lost the baby a week later. It would've been all I had left of him, now that's gone too." She said sadly.

Trying to change the subject, but she can't, "But that's over right; it's a new day now. I just can't understand how and why, it still hurts like hell, as if it just happened today!" Candy starts to cry softly. Tyrone gets up from the table walks over to her and kneels in front of her to hold her. She lays her head on his shoulder and cries.

"I'm sorry ma, I shouldn't of brought dis up. That was so stupid of me; I never want to see you cry! I'm sorry ma, I'm sorry. Come on, let's get dressed and go do something, get up out of here, and get some fresh air or something. Let's do something. I can't stand to see you like dis!" He tries to cheer her up.

She lifts her head from his shoulder and he kisses her. They later get dressed to go out on the town.

Hollywood, California

Tyler is in his office talking to his secretary Sherri. "Sherri, can I see you for a moment in my office?" He says over the speaker phone. "Sure Mr. Chapman, I'll be right in." She responds. As she enters his office, she asks, "Yes, Mr. Chapman, you wanted to see me?"

"Yes Sherri, come in, and please, call me Tyler." He reminds her. Smiling she says, "I'm sorry- 'Tyler,' how can I help you? "Sherri, I need you to do a little investigation work for me. I need you to find out everything you can on a Mr. Randle Emmitt. Find out where he's from and what he's into. "His family," friends- whatever!" Tyler explains.

"Also I need Gary Chandler's financial statements and his life insurance policy information. Whatever I ask you to do for this office Sherri stays in this office. You don't have to worry about the work you put into getting what I need, just know this, to be an investigator- you must also be paid like an investigator. Just let me know anything you need to make this happen, and I will make sure you get it."

"O.K, I can do that, and you don't ever have to worry about me Mr. - I mean Tyler, I love doing things for you. I would never break your trust." She reassures him. "Great Sherri, I knew I could count on you. I need this as soon as you can get it to me. I have a good feeling you're be sitting in your own big office real soon!" He says as he leans back in his chair smiling deviously, looking out the window.

It had only been two days into the New Year, and destruction was greatly upon mankind. The mere guilt and shame of their mortal actions has caused great suffering within themselves. Unaware of the consequences of their unguided decisions, they continuously journey towards a rapid destruction led by their own desires. A festival for Hell in the absence of God.

One Week Later

New Hope, Virginia

Grandma Ames and her daughter Brenda aged 32, are in the grocery store shopping. Brenda pushes the shopping buggy while walking beside her mother. Brenda says, "Look mama, the strawberries are nice and red today." "They sho are, must be the season for 'em."

Grandma Ames says in her distinct Southern accent. "Mama, we can't forget the bacon this time, I sho miss your bacon." Brenda smiles, Grandma Ames lets out a laugh, "Girl go on from here, you say that for just 'bout everything I cook." "Well it's true." Brenda laughs.

They walk down the store aisle laughing, suddenly, three men waving guns come in off the streets to rob the grocery store. The gunman shouts, "ALRIGHT! EVERYBODY ON THE FLOOR! Take off all yo jewelry and put it on the floor beside you. MOVE IT! And don't get fancy...or you're going to get smoked!"

In a panic, Brenda screams, "Oh My God Mama, what are we gonna do?" Always calm, Grandma Ames tells Brenda, "Just do what he say baby, the devil is mad." "But mama, we ain't got no jewelry!" Brenda says in distress. "We don't need no jewelry baby, we got Jesus!" Grandma Ames says firmly.

The three gunmen take over the entire grocery store, making everyone in the store get face down on the floor or against the walls.

Brenda and Grandma Ames were standing against the wall near the back of the store. After the gunmen make their rounds collecting the jewelry, they made their way to the back where Brenda and Grandma Ames are standing.

The second gunman yells angrily, "Ok old woman your turn, give it up!" Brenda tells the gunman, "You best leave my mama alone!" The gunman yells back, "B*&%$ you best shut your f#@%in mouth before I put a bullet in it! Now like I said, hand it over old lady!" Grandma Ames tells him, "Baby, I ain't got nothing to give you but Jesus." The gunman snaps back, "We don't give a f*#k about no Jesus, just hand over the money B#@!h!"

Grandma tells the gunman again, "Baby, I done told you, I ain't got nothing to give you." Now the gunman is really pissed off, "First of all I'm not yo f#%&in baby! So stop calling me dat! You came in dis f#%&in store to shop, so where is yo f#%&in shopping money." Grandma Ames says, "Mister, I don't shop wit real money, I use stamps."

Then the first gunman yells, "Everybody can't be using stamps in dis motherf$#@er!" nobody's going anywhere until somebody give up the f#%&in money!" Nobody says a word, about five minutes pass, and the gunmen are getting restless. One of the shoppers stands up and states, "There's more of us then there are of them, we can take them if we join together!" Everyone thinks about what the man said.

Without God's Grace and Mercy, they reacted on their own anger.

"HE'S RIGHT! Let's kill those sons of b&*$#@s!" Another shopper says. Everybody starts to chant, KILL THEM- KILL THEM- KILL THEM- KILL THEM- The people in the store go wild, the gunmen start shooting as the people attack the gunmen. It turns into a huge riot in the grocery store.

As fate would have it, the people began to turn on each other for no reason. They forget who and why they're fighting so they start fighting each other. The three gunmen were dead, along with a lot of innocent bystanders. Several people take the gunmen's guns and begin shooting in every direction. Bullets are flying everywhere in the store, the chance of anyone surviving is slim to none.

Grandma Ames grabs her daughter by the arm and leads her to a corner of the store. They sit on the floor and begin to go to a quiet place in the spirit. Grandma Ames begins to sing and Brenda joins her. As Grandma Ames looks up towards Heaven, she sings; "Your Grace and Mercy brought me through, I'm living this moment because of you, I want to thank you and praise you too, your Grace and Mercy brought me through."

Brenda also looks up towards Heaven and joins in with her. Within five minutes of singing, their ears were shut and the room becomes silent, they can see the chaos, but don't hear a sound, they see people being hit by stray bullets, but not one bullet comes near them.

They see people killing each other, and all of the horrific deaths, but nothing is able to disturb their peace in the spirit. Grandma Ames and her daughter just kept singing. Three hours later, everyone in the room except Grandma Ames and her daughter Brenda was dead.

Coming out of their quiet place their hearing returns, they stand up and step over many of the dead bodies and walk out of the building without a scratch. Within minutes of their departure, the police show up at the scene.

The next day, local television station 'News Watch 6', tells the grisly details of what happened. "Yesterday in New Hope, Virginia, the local police of Watts County discover over 190 shoppers dead in the town's grocery store without explanation. Every station covered the deadly story in their own way.

Even the Spanish language TV station has the story, Cuando Cien 90 pueblo fundar muerto en el este de Virginia y...

Brooklyn, New York

Tyrone is at Mike's house chilling watching TV. "Man you see this s#it, some people in a grocery store in Virginia got f$#@ed up! They said all those muthaf*&#ers were found dead! What kinda s%it is that?" Mike asks. Tyrone is in the kitchen getting a beer from the refrigerator, "Where you see dat at?" He says.

"It's all over the f#%&in news cuz. Man can you imagine every muthaf#@*er in the godd$#n store dead?" Tyrone says in disbelief, "Naw cuz, dat's sum bull&*$t!"

"Somebody did some-thing! Ain't nobody just gonna drop dead in the f#%&in grocery store; it's some mo s#it behind dat!" Mike responds, "I don't know cuz, just last week in Washington somewhere, a whole f#%&in church full of m*&$#@$#ers got burned to the ground. Man, that s#it is crazy!" Tyrone sits on the couch, and agrees, "For real- for real!"

Tyrone changes the conversation, "So Mike, what's up with you and Sonja, I heard y'all was kicking it hard?" Mike still looking at the TV, "We alright; she good people. I mean it ain't nothing serious- serious, not like you and ole girl." Tyrone leans back on the couch, "Aw here you go! "Why it got to be like me and ole girl?"

Mike teases, "You know you been hitting that!" Tyrone explains in a serious tone, "Actually I haven't, we just been chilling. She got a lot going on with her."

"I'm just trying to be that friend dat she can lean on." Mike isn't buying it, "Yeah right, a friend my a@s. Man, ain't no way I could have a honey dat fine lean on me, and I don't lean back." Tyrone breaks it down for Mike, "You see there Mike, dat's the difference between you and me. I ain't gotta be all up in a honey to be her friend. Dat's yo thang cuz."

"Hold up, stop the f#%&in press, you fo real about dat girl! Boy as long as I've known you, I ain't never heard you talk about a girl like dat.

It's all good doe, I'm happy for y'all, somebody had to step in and take control of dat damsel in distress." Mike says. "It ain't even like dat cuz, but I'ma let you have dat." Tyrone replies. "So where she at now? Y'all ain't hooking up today?"

Tyrone explains, "Na, she went to see her shrink about not being able to let her man go. She's really taken it bad cuz. The other day she started screaming in her sleep like somebody just told her about it cuz.

I didn't know what to do! I woke her up and she started talking crazy. She called me dat nigga's name and started saying s#it like-'I promise you baby, I'm gonna find the nigga who did dis to you!' I don't know dog, I hope she do find that nigga, I'ma help her f#@k dat nigga up, for what he did to her. Man, this s#it is crazy."

Atlanta, Georgia

Rhonda and her mother are in the doctor's office waiting room. Rhonda is holding her mother's hand and shaking her leg, nervously. "Ma, I'm scared, what if the doctor tells me that I got it?"

What am I gonna to do ma, what am I gonna do?" She asks. Holding her daughter's hand and praying, "I don't know baby, but we will deal with it somehow, I promise you- I will do everything- I will find the best medical specialists in Georgia or where ever!"

Sadly she says, "God, if you would've just listened to me about that boy, it was something about him that I just didn't like. I knew he was no good. He just had that look about him; I could just kill him for what he's putting you through."

Rhonda feeling bad, "I know ma, I already feel bad about all this, you're right- I should've listened- but I didn't and here we are!" "Aw baby, I'm not mad at you, I'm just so d#@n mad about this whole mess. I'm going to talk to his parents and if you so much as caught a cold from that nasty boy, I am going to sue the pants off of them!"

The front desk nurse pages, "Rhonda Johnson the doctor will see you now." Rhonda and her mother follow the nurse to the examination room. "Don't worry baby everything's going to be alright." Her mother reassures her. Rhonda shaking nervously nods her head with teary eyes.

They wait in the examination room for 30 minutes before the doctor comes in. "Hello, my name is Doctor Sonal, and you must be- he looks down at his chart, "Ms. Johnson, it's my pleasure to meet you." Glancing at his chart, "I see you're here for testing, why do you feel you need to be tested?" Dr. Sonal asks. Ashamed, "I think my boyfriend- I mean- ex-boyfriend, gave me a virus." The Doctor asks, "What virus are we talking about?" Rhonda hesitates, "Uh- the- AIDS virus."

A concerned look comes over Dr. Sonal's face, "I see! I take it you never thought of protecting yourself?" Rhonda replies, "Actually, I did- but- he told me that he was straight." Dr.Sonal frowns, "and you believed him? Are you aware that 92% of young girls like yourself have come in contact with the virus, because somebody carrying it around said that they are straight?

I see this every day, no one really thinks about protecting themselves, until it's too late." Mom jumps in the conversation, "I tried to warn her about that boy doctor, but these young kids today just seem to do whatever they want to do, I don't know what to do." Dr. Sonal responds, "Well, there's not much you can do, we can't be with them 24/7."

"Well, Nurse Ramsey is going to do some blood work and we'll test you for everything known to man and pray everything's negative. Would you like your mother to stay with you while they do the blood work?" With tears in her eyes, Rhonda says, "I want her to stay."

"Ok then, when she's done with you, I'll be back with the results shortly." as the Doctor is leaving the room. "You mean to tell me that you can test her today and have the results back in the same day?" mom asks? "Absolutely" The technology today is quite advanced." says Dr. Sonal.

"Wow, that's amazing. So then, why can't they come up with a cure for AIDS?" mom asks. "They have, the problem is, no one can afford it, and insurance doesn't cover it." Explains Dr. Sonal, "That's a d$#n shame! How can they say that they're trying to save the people when they won't even help heal them?" Tammy asks.

The Doctor explains, "Ms. Johnson, in case you haven't noticed, the world is a cruel and ungodly place these days. People are more concerned about themselves. It's quite difficult to find compassion within anyone in this time." Shaking her head, "You're sure right about that doctor."

Dr. Sonal says, "Nurse Ramsey will take it from here and then you'll see me again. I hope for the best for you Ms. Johnson." "Thank you doctor." Tammy says.

After a few minutes, Nurse Ramsey comes in and starts the blood work. The process lasts about 30 minutes. After several blood tests are completed, they proceed back to the examination room to wait for the doctor to return with the results.

"Baby, I think I'm about to lose my mind up in here, I don't know what I'm going to do if these results don't come back right!" Tammy says. "You" "How do you think I feel? I mean, my life and future will be gone mama, gone!" as Rhonda starts to cry, Mom tries to console her daughter. "Don't say that baby, we're going to make it through this, one way or another, and if it takes everything that I have baby, I'm going to make sure that you have a future. I promise you that!" They both hold each other crying.

About an hour later Dr. Sonal returns with her results. By this time Rhonda and her mother have regained their composure, but are still on edge. Dr. Sonal says, "Ms. Johnson, there's no easier way to say this, but, not only do you have the virus, you are also pregnant. Along with the AIDS virus, we also discovered Herpes, syphilis, chlamydia, and gonorrhea. Apparently whoever did this to you was highly aware of his condition, because everything is at its worst stages. In addition, the other virus amplifies the AIDS virus.

Dr. Sonal takes a deep breath, "This is truly a very rare case and I highly recommend a medical campus. There you will get all the assistance you'll need to cure some and fight the others. However if you refuse, I give you less than one year to live." Tammy lets out a loud cry, as passes out in the floor. "NURSE! I NEED SOME ASSISTANCE HERE!" yells Dr. Sonal.

The doctor and his nurse lift Tammy to the examination table trying to help her regain consciousness. Rhonda slides down the wall behind them talking to herself. "You mean, as she cries, I'm going to die- I'm going to die-sobbing, he killed me- he took my life- he took my future- and- all I did was love him- and he- took my life!"

With eyes full of tears, she stands up and walks over to the cabinet in the examination room, she opens it and sees a scalpel, and without thought slices her own throat. Hearing the bump from her fall, Dr. Sonal turns away from her mother and sees gushing blood from Rhonda's neck.

Dr. Sonal panics, "OH MY GOD! WHAT HAVE YOU DONE! OH NO! NO! The Nurse screams. Dr. Sonal yells "Nurse, Nurse! Call the ambulance! Quickly! Quickly!" Securing his gloves, Dr Sonal firmly places a towel on Rhonda's neck to the slit across her throat as he tries to stop the bleeding. While attending to Rhonda on the floor, her mother regains consciousness on the examination table. She looks over and sees the doctor with a towel to her daughter's neck and the blood gushing through the towel.

Tammy lets out a loud scream at the top of her lungs, "NOOOOO!- NO!"As she holds her head, she falls to the floor and slowly moves around the doctor, who's still applying pressure to the bad wound. Crawling to her daughter's body, she grabs her hand screaming, "Rhonda!- Rhonda- NO, AHHHH-

NOT MY RHONDA- NOOOO- AHHHHH- OH MY BABY- NOT MY BABY- NO- NO- AHHH- RHONDAAAA- AHHHH- NOOOOO!'" With her hands covered in her daughter's blood, she lays her face on her unconscious daughter's stomach and cries.

Hollywood, California

Three days later

In the living room, Susan is on the couch looking at the big screen TV watching the news and sipping on a cup of coffee, Tyler walks in the room about to leave for work. "What are you watching?", Tyler asks? "Wow, some girl in Atlanta just slit her throat in a doctor's office!" Susan replies.

"Wow! When did this happen?" Tyler asks. "I think about two or three days ago, they said that everybody was disturbed about it, the doctor- the nurse- the girl's mother- everybody!" She says.

"This happened in Atlanta?" Susan responds, "Yes Atlanta, Georgia. "Oh my god, I would have freaked out if I would've been in that doctor's office that day. I wonder if he'll continue practicing after all this." Tyler replies, "of course he will; as a doctor, I'm sure he's seen a lot worse in his day!"

"I certainly wouldn't give up my practice for someone else's problem. Let them deal with it, it's not his drama it's theirs!" Tyler says dismissively. Sarcastically, Susan says, "Yeah, I almost forgot how compassionate you are!" Tyler responds, "C'mon Susan, compassion has nothing to do with it, business is business."

"Compassion will only keep you broke, of course that's not a word you would understand, yet." Susan asks, "And what is that supposed to mean?" "Exactly what it sounds like- Yet!" Tyler exclaims. Susan gets off the couch with her cup of coffee; my father- Tyler angrily interrupts her, "YOUR FATHER WHAT! The only thing your father better do is watch his back, lately he seems to be biting off more than he can chew!"

Stunned because of Tyler's aggressive tone, Susan says, "You're not making any sense, Tyler. My father never does anything he can't handle!" Tyler walks out the door, "That's what he wants you to believe!"

Seattle, Washington

Karen, the former wife of the late Pastor Charles, is in the kitchen making lunch when she hears a knock at her front door. It's a Washington State police officer. "Yes, who is it?" Asks Karen, "It's the State Police ma'am!" the officer says in a deep voice. Suddenly, nervous she says "O-ok- just a moment." Karen looks in the mirror to quickly prep her hair and face, then walks to the door.

Opening the door, she inquires, "How can I help you officer?" "Hello ma'am, I'm officer Sykes, I'm looking for a Mrs. Karen Palmer, the wife of a Charles Palmer." Nervously she responds, "That's- that's me. Is there a problem officer?" "I'm sorry to have to inform you ma'am that your husband Charles Palmer is deceased. It seems that he was trapped in a church fire a few days ago. At this time we're unaware of the causes for the fire, but forensics has identified some of the remains and among those identified was your husband, Charles. We were told that he was the Pastor there, is this true?"

Leaning against the door frame with tears running from her eyes, shocked at the confirmation of her husband's death, she stutters, "Yes- yes- ha- he was- he was the pastor there." "Again I'm sorry for your loss ma'am; I really hate this for you. If there's anything we can do just let us know. We'll keep you posted concerning the causes and whatever else we can find. Here's my card, if you have any questions just give us a call."

Almost fainting, Karen says, "Thank you officer." You try and take it easy today ma'am, goodbye. In a whisper, Karen says, "bye!" She slowly closes the door as the officer walks away. With her hands behind her, holding the door knob, she leans her head back on the door and silently cries from her soul.

Brooklyn, New York

Candy is on the couch at her psychiatrist, Amy Mathews' office. "Ok Candy, let's go over this again, let's see, you've been having the same recurring dream for the past 6 months and nothing seems to be getting any better. Why do you think you're having these dreams and what do you think causes them, she asks?"

Candy starts to cry as if she just heard the news about her boyfriend's death. "I don't know why I keep having these dreams, but I do know that they are more than just dreams. They are visions or- or warnings or something, I don't know!" Candy says.

"Warnings, what sort of warnings, do you feel that some kind of supernatural thing is happening to you or something" asks Amy? Candy quickly looks up at her as if she said something profound, "Then you do understand- at -at first I- I just thought it was a stupid idea or- I don't know.

But then it just kept happening and all I could hear was Tony saying to me, 'find my killer', it's like he's trying to tell me who it was or something-I -I don't know- I just- I just gotta find him- I gotta know who did this to him, I want to know what he looks like and then I want to put a bullet through his head in the same- in same way he did my Tony!"

Candy is shaking, holding her head with her fingers through her hair. "Candy, she says calmly, "You do realize what you are saying right? You're talking about taking someone's life."

"This is very serious. I mean how would you know who it was, or what this person even looks like?"

"Hypothetically speaking, what if you found out it was someone you knew or someone you care about, would you feel the same? Could you put a bullet through their head as well?" she asks.

Candy looks down slowly as if she's in a daze, "I don't know, I- I never thought of it that way, I guess- I would have to, I mean- I- I know that's what he would want me to do! It- it has to be- because- why else would he be in my dreams all this time?" Amy slowly reaches for her silent emergency button under her chair, "Just relax Candy, it's all going to be ok, I'm going to do everything I can do to help you, you just have to trust me, and know that I will never do anything to ever hurt you."

As she stands up, two tall, muscular orderlies enter the office, dressed in white uniforms. Candy sees them and asks, "What's going on, this is a private session, why are they here?" Amy replies, "Its ok Candy, they are just here to help you."

In a rage, Candy screams, "HELP ME!, HELP ME HOW? YOU THINK I'M CRAZY DON'T YOU? You think I've lost my mind- I trusted you with my thoughts and dreams, and you want to have me admitted- Are you serious?"

"Listen to me Candy, no one here wants to hurt you, we just don't want you to hurt yourself or anybody else! We have the best doctors available for you, who can help you through this. You don't have to do this alone anymore!"

In a rage, Candy yells, "help me through this, that's what I thought you were doing!

What the hell do you mean I don't have to do this alone anymore, I was never alone, I have my boyfriend Tyrone, and a lot of other friends, one in which I thought was you! I don't have to take this, you can't keep me here, I'm leaving and I'm not going to see no d%#n doctor either! You can just go to hell-get out of my way!" She pushes past Amy.

Amy shouts, "Orderlies! I'm sorry Candy we can't let you do that, when someone admits to wanting to pre-meditate a murder, we have to take them into custody to prevent the actual crime!" Candy yells, "Get your f#%&in hands OFF ME!- NO!- NO!- YOU CAN'T- MAKE ME GO- WITH YOU!

Kicking and screaming, "LEAVE ME ALONE YOU BASTARDS! LEAVE ME ALONE! STOP-STOP- NO!- YOU HAVE NO RIGHT TO DO THIS TO ME! PLEASE- SOMEBODY- HELP ME!- TOOOOOOONY!"

Atlanta, Georgia

At her daughter's funeral, Tammy sees several of Rhonda's school friends. Family members, from across the country, come to pay their respects to Rhonda. Tammy's brother, Robert from Connecticut, sits beside her, on the front row, with his arm around her, trying to console her, at the church where the family attends. Their pastor gives the eulogy, and one of the choir members sings the timeless song, Amazing Grace.

It's a very sad moment for everyone, especially Rhonda's mother Tammy. In her mind, her world as she knew it is over. The one chance to fulfill the promise she made to her daughter about the security of her future, is shattered into thousands of pieces. Her heart is overwhelmed with grief. The funeral lasts three hours. Leaving the church, the spectators follow the hearse to the cemetery.

Everyone is gathered beneath and around the tent at the burial plot. Seeing her daughter's coffin, she becomes weak in the knees and nearly passes out. Her brother Robert catches her and helps her to her seat. After a few words from the Pastor, another emotional song is sung, the body is lowered into the ground and everyone heads back to Tammy's house for the reception.

Two hours later, everyone is at Tammy's house eating and mingling. Tammy tries her best to keep a straight face and not show her true feelings, until a special uninvited guest appears at her home. Tammy is out on her back patio reflecting, she needed some time alone.

She hears a woman's voice asking for her. "Pardon me, I'm looking for Tammy Johnson." the lady says. She was talking to Tammy's brother, but didn't know it. "Are you a friend?" Robert asked.

"No, not really, we haven't formally met yet. I believe we have a lot in common, because I just lost my son as well, and I wanted to pay my respects to her." She says.

Robert replies, "I'm sorry to hear that, thank you so much for coming, let me get her for you." Robert goes to the patio to tell Tammy about the woman who wants to talk to her.

"There you are; there's a young lady inside who wants to meet you and give her respects. You want me to bring her out here to you, or do you want to come in and talk to her?" asks Robert. Tammy asks, "Who is she?" "I don't know, she said that you two haven't formally met yet, she feels you two have something in common." Tammy tells her brother, "You can tell her to come out here, cause I'm really not up to being around a crowd right now."

"I can understand that, ok I'll send her out." her brother says. "Thanks Robert and thanks so much for coming, I don't think I could have done this without you." Tammy says. "You don't have to thank me, we're family, that's my niece, and you're my baby sister, nothing could've stopped me from being here for you, I love you girl." He hugs her, she cries on his shoulder.

"I love you too big brother, love you too." Tammy says. "Let me go get this woman so she can share her story with you, maybe she can bring a mutual smile to your face." "I doubt it, but it's worth a try." She says with a half- smile.

Robert leaves the patio to find the woman. "Hi again, my sister is on the patio, she wants you to come out there to talk to her. By the way, what's your name?" Robert asks. "I'm sorry for being so rude, I should've introduced myself, I'm just a bit disturbed about all of this."

"I'm Regina, I live across town, and I just heard about this on the news a few days ago, I just had to come." She says. "Well again, thank you for coming. The patio is to your left, you will find her out there", Robert says.

Regina walks to the patio. Entering the patio she sees Tammy facing the back yard looking towards the sky. "Excuse me, are you Tammy?" Regina asks. Tammy turns around to look at her. "Yes, I'm Tammy and who are you?" "My name is Regina. I wanted to stop by to pay my respects. I just recently lost my son, and I know how you feel. I heard about your daughter on the news a few days ago, and it reminded me so much of my own son, so much that I had to meet you." She says.

"I am sorry to hear about your son and yes, it is hard for me right now. She was my everything- my only child. I just can't imagine my life without her." Tammy says sadly. About to cry, Regina says emotionally, "I do understand, my son was my only child, and when he died, I died inside."

"He was all I had- when his father left us, he became very bitter and blamed me for him leaving."

"I tried to make him understand, that it wasn't my fault, but he held that against me- to the point that he turned to another man. A man who gave him AIDS. Pausing briefly, she continues, and god only knows what else. So when I heard about your daughter and her condition, it made me think about my son. That's why I had to meet you." She explains. "It's ironic how our children died with the same disease. Was your son aware of what he had?" Tammy asks.

"Yes, this happened about three years ago", Regina says. "How did you handle it, did you get any kind of medical help for him?" Tammy asks. "I tried, but everything I did wasn't a concern of his, because of how he felt about me, so he refused to go. I tried to force him, but he would just run away and hide for days."

"He hasn't lived with me for almost two years. He moved across town to stay with his father. He just kept ignoring the problem as if it would just go away. He showed up to school whenever he wanted too, and if he didn't want to he wouldn't go.

His father never made him do anything he didn't want to do. When I found out that he was deliberately sleeping around- mad at the world for his mistakes, I called the police and they arrested him and made him get some medical help, but it was a while before they caught up with him. It's no telling how many girls he infected before they caught him.

"What did you say your name was?" Regina? Regina- Bryant. Tammy thinks, "Bryant, Bryant- that name sounds so familiar, what was your son's name?" "My son's name was Terry- Terry Bryant, why, did you know him?"

Tammy becomes ragingly angry, "DID I KNOW HIM! THAT BASTARD KILLED MY DAUGHTER! I TRIED TO WARN MY DAUGHTER ABOUT THAT SON OF A B$#@h BUT SHE WOULDN'T LISTEN, and YOU- you have the audacity to come to my home talking about your dead son, you better be glad he's dead, because I was on my way to kill him after my daughter's funeral anyway!

YOUR SON, CAN ROT IN HELL AS FAR AS I AM CONCERNED, AND YOU BETTER WATCH YOUR BACK B&*#h BECAUSE YOU'RE NEXT ON MY LIST!"

"How can you say that, I'm not responsible for my son's actions, what he did was wrong, but why blame me for his wrong doings" Regina asks. "Because you birthed that son of a b$#@h, that's why!" Regina stutters, "h- h- HOW DARE YOU!"

"I can show you better than I can tell you b&$#h!" Tammy grabs a large flower pot nearby and throws it at her, hitting her in the head. Regina falls to the floor bleeding, trying to get up, Tammy stomps her in the stomach four times and then straddles her body punching her.

Regina, bruised, is trying to fight back, but can't seem to get in a punch. Hearing all the commotion on the patio, Robert and some of the guests come out to see what's going on. Seeing Regina on the floor with blood all over her, he grabs his sister and pulls her off Regina.

"WHAT THE HELL IS GOING ON!" Robert yells. Kicking and screaming as he holds her back, "THAT B*$#h KILLED MY DAUGHTER!" Everyone becomes silent trying to hear more.

"What! What are you talking about Tammy", Robert asks surprised. "Rhonda killed herself!" Tammy yells, "NO SHE DIDN'T, IT WAS HER BASTARD SON WHO GAVE MY

DAUGHTER THAT Da%n DISEASE!" "Oh my god" Roberts says, still restraining his sister. "Lady- I think you better leave, and never show your face at this house again!" Robert advises Regina.

Some of the guests help her from the floor and out the door. Another guest offers to take her to the hospital. Everyone was in a state of shock and Tammy was still in a rage. Robert releases his hold on his sister Tammy, "Ok-ok-she's gone calm down- everything is alright now!"

Tammy snatches away from her brothers hands, "All Right- all right! It ain't even close to being alright- but this is one promise I can keep- I promise you- it will be!" Seeking revenge.

Chapter 5

Hollywood, California

The Plan

Early morning, Tyler is in his office working. His secretary calls for him on the speaker phone. "Mr. Chapman, may I speak to you for a moment." Tyler responds, "Of course Sherri, come right in." Sherri enters his office, "I just wanted to let you know that I have the information you requested from me. I must say it wasn't easy. I had to pull a few strings, but in the end I got it done." She says proudly.

"You're an amazing woman Sherri, I am beginning to wonder why I didn't meet you first- eight years ago before I met my wife!" he laughs. Sherri laughs nervously, "I'm sure you don't mean that Mr. Chapman. Mrs. Chapman is quite the woman herself. I mean from where I stand, I could never fill her shoes, even if I tried- I mean, don't get me wrong- I'm not trying-I um- I'm- I'm just saying." Tyler says, "It's ok Sherri, you don't have to worry, I'm in no danger of you becoming like my wife. In fact, if I was, I think I would have fired you quite some time ago!"

Feeling a little awkward, she says "Ok- wow! I guess that's good to know." "I'm sorry, but I might as well be for real about this thing. I mean, Sherri between you and I, my wife is JUST a wife! I've never loved that woman since the day I met her scumbag father, whom I despise with all my heart."

"His way of stepping over people and pushing them out of his way; just isn't something I find amusing." He explains. "Getting what he wants regardless of the consequences was his way of fanning his money in everyone's face. At least that's the way he use to do it, before I started doing the stomping! Now amazingly enough, he's dancing to my beat; a beat that will cost him everything!" Looking out the window in deep thought, "Maybe even his life, it just depends on how I feel!"

A moment of silence comes over the office. "Wow! I didn't know it was so intense. So, if you don't mind me asking, why are you still with Mrs. Chapman if you don't or, didn't love her?" Sherri asks.

"I don't mind at all Sherri, ask me anything. However the answer to your question is quite obvious. M-O-N-E-Y! He had it- I wanted it- and until I could find a way to get it- she was my access to it! However, now that the ball is in my court, I really don't need her anymore!" Stunned, Sherri says, "Wow, I've actually seen movies about stuff like this- but never in real life." Tyler asks, "Movies like what Sherri?" Sherri stumbles, "You know like- movies were the husband might knock off this wife's lover for the money- or somebody hires a hitman to take out his father-in-law- or wife or somebody- I don't know- I do watch some pretty strange stuff sometimes. I guess that's why I don't take a lot of things serious."

Thinking hard, "You know, you just might have something there Sherri!" Tyler says. Facing his window, with one arm folded, and the other hand on his chin, he says "This could be the solution to my little problem. Yeah! It just might work!"

Turning around quickly, he says, "Sherri, get my wife on the phone and tell her I said to dress up in her finest outfit, tell her I'll be sending a car to pick her up. Oh yeah, order some roses and have them delivered to the house, today."

Looking totally confused, Sherri says, "I thought you said that she- you- didn't want- Tyler interrupts her, "Sherri, I'm surprised at you, being a woman and all. I mean, weren't you aware, that's the way to a fool's money is through their heart. I mean at least I- still think I have what it takes to woo a woman, what do you think?"

In total disbelief of what she's hearing, "I- I guess so-uh- I- Tyler interrupts her again, by quickly pulling her body to his and passionately kissing her without warning. Tyler slowly pulls away and looks deviously in her eyes, "Hold that thought, you're my part two!"

Seattle, Washington

Karen is in the living room watching TV when she gets a call from one of her former members about their church, having to answer questions that she has no insight on, causing unexpected results. The phone rings, Karen answers "yes?" "Sister Palmer, God bless you, it's been so long since we've spoke, I just wanted to touch bases with you and see how you are doing." The caller says.

"Sister Gloria, how have you been, I was just thinking about you on yesterday. How's the family? Are you ok, do you need anything" Karen asks?" "No ma'am Sister Palmer, we are all just fine, thank you for asking. Some of the other members and me just wanted to know what happened to Pastor Palmer. We heard that he was found burned up in the church, what happened?"

Taking a deep breath and starting to get a little shaky, Karen says "I- I really don't know the whole story myself'; only what I've heard from the police, which was the same as what you've heard." "You mean to tell me that they couldn't tell you anything about your husband's death. I mean, what was he doing in the church on a Monday morning anyway? Bible Study is on Wednesday's." She says. Karen remembers the fire she set at the church, "I-I really can't answer that, I- I don't know- I guess it's a- mystery to all of us."

"Mystery is right, I mean there were a lot of things that Pastor started doing that was quite mysterious to a lot of us!" Sister Gloria says.

"What do you mean things like what?" Sister Gloria explains. "Well, I'm not the dog to carry the bone, but just know that there were some things about Pastor, that we all noticed that just didn't set right with us!"Karen's searching for answers. "Certainly I would never view you as a dog carrying a bone, however, I would like to know of that in which you are speaking of."

"Sister Palmer, we go way back, as far back as the initial opening of the church and in all those years, Pastor has been Pastor to me. However as of lately, there were things that were said and done, that turned our faces against Pastor. That was the reason Sister Martha and Sister Sarah pulled away from the alter worker position. The only reason I stayed there, was because of you. I knew you didn't know, and I love you so much that I certainly didn't want to hurt you, or be the one to tell you the truth!" She explains the situation.

Karen curiously asks, "Be the one to tell me what truth, about what? "I swore to myself that I would never tell you this, but since Pastor is gone now, I don't see the harm in telling you. Remember that night Pastor called the alter call, in fact it was the last alter call he made.

Anyway, I was the one working the altar beside him that night, when that floozy walked up to him supposedly giving her prayer request!", says Sister Gloria. "I remember that night, I remember feeling sick or something when she walked up there, I don't know-something just didn't feel right!" Karen remembers.

"That feeling that you had was your discerning spirit alerting you of the devil himself", says Sister Gloria. When she slithered down to the altar up in his face, I could see the devil all over her. She thought I didn't hear her, but it was as if God opened my ears to what they both were saying to each other.

She told him that she wanted him to touch her and ease her lonely pain, and he tried to whisper back to her telling her that he would take care of her problem after church in his office. Remember when you came in the hallway and saw me arguing with Pastor in front of his office door, and when you walked up, he said that he was just trying to tell me the proper place to stand when he's ministering? I swear I thought you knew something wasn't right. I mean, come on, all those years I've stood by him at that alter, and all of a sudden my placement is wrong, really?"

Karen says in disbelief, "All this time I thought it was just your placement. Oh Gloria, I was so naïve. I guess I was so in-love with that man that I could see no wrong in him. How could I have been so blind? So that's why he kept telling me to go on home ahead of him, he said that he had a lot of paper work to finish up before Sunday morning service. Oh, I feel so stupid!"

I shook her hand and hugged her after service that night, because she came to me telling me how much the service blessed her soul. My God! I remember feeling like I needed to wash up after she hugged me, but I just wrote it off as a sign of my flesh crawling due to a lack of rest. I didn't want to believe it was any one person."

Sister Gloria tells her, "Sister Karen I am so sorry to have had to be the one to tell you all this, but just know, it was your true walk with God that kept the majority of the members in the church all these years, me included. I had to repent myself, because I continued to stand by him at that alter, knowing what he did with that woman behind your back and in the sight of God."

I humbly ask for your forgiveness, because I myself am a true woman of God, and will never do anything to ever intentionally hurt or disrespect you at any cost. I'm so sorry."

With tears in her eyes, Karen says, "I forgive you, although there really isn't a reason for you to feel bad about not wanting to hurt me. I respect your decision not to tell me. I mean sometimes it's easier to hear it when God relays it to you, so thank you." Sister Gloria then says,

"Well, this is certainly not the reason why I called you, but I guess it was the right time to get it off my heart. I've troubled you long enough today, so I'm going to let you go now but I will be in touch from time to time to check up on you. I love you so much Sister Palmer and you be blessed. Bye, bye now."

Karen replies, "Oh, you were no trouble at all Gloria, I'm just glad to finally know the truth. I am glad that you called and that you released this burden from your heart. You take care and do keep in touch; it's always a pleasure to hear from you. God bless you... good bye."

Hanging up the phone Karen falls to her knees with her face to the floor and cries from her soul. Later that evening, while lying in her bed, her phone rings. "Hello- hello- hello is anyone there?" She asks. A raspy voice almost that of a whisper says, "Hello darling, did you miss me?" Frustrated, Karen says, "Who is this and why are you whispering?" The voice on the phone says, "Ooooh- I'm hurt, you forgot me already, well my love, I haven't forgotten you."

Getting more upset by the minute, Karen says, "I don't know who you are, but don't call this house again, or I will-interrupted by the voice, "You will what- burn me up again?"

Hearing that statement she says nervously, "Who- who is this?" "It's me baby, your husband Charles, just wanted you to know, that I'm coming home." Karen is shaking in fear, "Stop it- I don't know what- kind of games you're playing- but it's not amusing. Charles is dead so stop playing your stupid games and leave me alone!"

She hangs up the phone. She hears a noise coming from the living room. Karen grabs a bat from the closet that belonged to her husband, and slowly moves towards the door. She quietly, opens the door and eases into the hallway, not thinking to turn on any lights. Hearing the noise again, she begins to shake even harder, almost dropping the bat.

As she slides her back against the wall that leads to the living room, she raises the bat above her shoulder in a swinging position.

Counting to three in her mind, she prepares to jump out from behind the wall swinging her bat at whatever moves.

Remembering the raspy voice made her very jumpy and scared, "help me God", she whispers to herself. She then senses a presence of someone or something on the other side of the wall, gripping the bat tightly with both hands, she leaps from behind the wall swinging and screaming. There was also the sound of screaming coming from the other presence as well, as the bat was snatched from her hands.

Falling to the floor she could only imagine the worst that could happen at that moment. The lights were switched on, and there stood her son with the bat in his hands and her daughter behind him screaming. Seeing their mother on the floor shaken, they rushed over to her. "Mother what's the matter with you, trying to hit me with this bat?" Her son Samuel says.

Standing by the door crying in fear, Rachael asks, "What's wrong with you, you scared the heck out of me, oh my God, why did you do that?" Karen lays on the floor shaking, unable to speak from the shock of her imagination.

"Mother are you alright, what's wrong with you, why are you shaking so hard?" Samuel asks. Picking her up from the floor, she falls into his arms crying saying, "It -it was him-it was Charles!" Samuel looking into his mother's eyes could tell that she was serious, but also thought she was just grieving over his death.

Still in shock of the scare, Rachael says "Mama, daddy's dead- what do you mean it was Charles?" Karen stares into space in a state of shock, "It-it was- it was him!"

New Hope, Virginia

Grandma Ames is in her bed half asleep when the spirit of God appears. "AMES! - AMES!" Stunned by the voice, Grandma Ames wonders if it's just in her mind or real. As she slowly recognizes the voice of God, she sits up in her bed, "Speak Lord thy servant hearth thee."

God responds, "I have seen your heart, I have found no greater faith among mankind then I have found in you. Your faith is strong, for this I have blessed you with the gift of sight. I have opened your eyes unto the world and placed you at the gates of their faith.

Your steps will be ordered, and your words will possess power. Neither Devil nor Demon will be able to destroy that which I have blessed you with. I the Living God will be with you. Ask and it shall be given unto you; when you seek me you will find me. For great is your mountain but I am your latter; neither look to your right nor to your left, but unto me and I will deliver. I have placed you upon a path in which no man has traveled before you; be not afraid for I am with you."

Your hands are made strong for the pulling down of strong holds. Many weapons will form, but I am your shield. Stand tall and be strong for your time is now! I the Living God have spoken and declare it by the heavens and by the earth and so shall it be!"

With her face to the floor, Grandma Ames says, "Be it unto me according to thy will!"

Atlanta, GA

Tammy is lying across her bed watching TV, when she gets a call from a friend. "Hello, oh hey girl what's up?" Tammy asks. "Nothing much, what chu doing?" the caller asks. "Nothing, just laying here watching TV, or should I say it's watching me" Tammy says. "Did your brother go home yet?" The caller inquires. "No, he's leaving tomorrow; he calls himself watching me, trying to make sure I don't do anything stupid he says! But he gotta go home sometimes." She says.

The caller laughs, "Stupid like what?" "I don't know girl, I guess he thinks I'm going to kill that b*&#h that killed my child!" Caller remembers. "Oh yeah, that's why I called you. What hospital did you say you work at?" Tammy replies. "Southern General," Why?" "I just got word that your girl is in the intensive care unit at that hospital, "Southern General! It seems that you gave ole girl a concussion with that big a## flower pot you hit her with."

Tammy replies, "Girl I tried to kill that b*&$h! If Robert would've stayed away for just five more minutes- we would not be having this conversation!" "Well, the way I see it, we don't have to have this conversation, if you were to go to work on your day off and handle that s%it."

"You know what; I knew there was something I liked about you, that sh%t just might work!" Thinking hard, "Hey, give me 10 minutes and then meet me behind Southern General! I gotta get dressed for work!" Tammy says!

Brooklyn, New York

Tyrone and Mike are driving to Candy's house, "Man I can't believe dat it's been three d#@n weeks since you've seen dis girl and you still expect her to talk to you." Mike says. Tyrone smiles, "Obviously cuz, you don't know what true love really is." "Obviously you don't either, if you think she gonna holla at you after three weeks." "Well like da say, actions speak louder den words, correct?" asked Tyrone.

"Well, dat all depends on who the hell "da," is, and did "da," wait three weeks to try to get sum action" smiles Mike. Tyrone laughs "you stupid cuz." They pull up in front of Candy's house, get out of the car and walk to her door. Tyrone rings the doorbell. "She might not be home cuz, I don't see her car." Mike laughs, "She might've saw you coming and got the hell on." "You got jokes", Tyrone states!

A fair skinned woman comes to the door and asks, "Can I help you?" Tyrone is shocked to see another person, he stutters, "uh, yeah-um-is Candy in?" The woman responds rudely, "No!" "Do you know where she at?" asks Tyrone. "Yep!" The woman says. "O-K, can you tell me, were she's at" asks Tyrone?

The woman replies, "Nope!" "Man, f%$k this b$#@h" dog, we ain't got time for dis sh*# man!" Mike says angrily. "Hold up cuz, there's gotta be a reason miss lady ain't feeling us, so let's just see what's up." Tyrone thinks. The woman tells Tyrone & Mike, "look I ain't got time fo dis sh#t, so do yo self a favor and get the f%$k off my porch!"

Tyrone says, "Hold up ma, you don't know me like dat! I didn't come here for your skanky a#@ anyway, I came to see my girl, so why don't you do yo self a favor and tell me where the hell she is and I'll be on my da#n way." "YO GIRL" Looking him up and down, "So you must be da nigga my daughter "F#%&in wit? Well, I guess you haven't heard?" Confused, Tyrone says, "Heard what? Hold up, YO DAUGHTER! What the f$#k? What the hell are you doing here, and where the hell is Candy?"

"That's what I'm trying to tell yo black a##" but you won't listen, she's in the hospital." The mother says. "Hospital" What da, what happened, is she hurt, is she all right? When did dis happen, what's up?" Tyrone asks. Calmly leaning against the doorway smoking a cigarette, the woman says "You done? She's not hurt at least not physically, she's out there."

"What da f$#k does out there mean?" The woman replies, just what it sounds like, out there, crazy- gone- going- or whatever you want to call it!"

Frustrated Tyrone asks, "Ok, can you give a straight gotda%n answer? what da hell does crazy, gone, going mean?" "Ok, it's like this, my beloved daughter isn't the brightest apple of the tree, I mean, she would rather date a thug, than to date decent men. She would rather run with losers then to get with a winner and she would rather get help from a dead man than from a live man like yourself."

In others words, they took her a@s away in a strait jacket when she decided to tell the man that she wanted to put a bullet- in the head- of her dead man's killer! And then called on her dead man for help when they drug her a## away!" She explains.

"Oh, and for the record, the reason I'm in her house, is because that little bi$#h stole my money out of my account to buy or rent a Motherf#%&in private-eye to find her man's killer! That money that she stole was my recovery money for my d$#n house! Which, may I add- I ended up losing; along with everything in it- because of dat sh#t. Now, her house is my house. So right about now, I don't give a da#n if that bi#@h rots in that mother$#@er, cause she ain't getting this sh#t back!"

"Daaaaam! Man dat's some wild sh#t", says Mike. Speechless and confused, Tyrone turns and walks back to the car, Mike follows him. "I'm really sorry dat you got mixed up in her sh#t, because you seem like a nice fellow!" She yells as they walk to the car. She turns to go back in the house and closes the door. Mike and Tyrone get back in the car. Mike drives around going nowhere in particular, giving Tyrone some time to his thoughts. Neither one says a word.

Hollywood, California

Tyler and his wife, Susan are out having dinner at an expensive restaurant. "I must say honey; you're looking quite beautiful tonight." Tyler flatters Susan." Smiling, "Well, thank you," "It's been so long since we've had a night out together," "It really feels good." "I just want us to work." She says looking seriously in his eyes. "I want us to be a family again." "I would do anything- whatever you want- however you want it- just to be one with you again," "I love you so much Tyler!"

Feeling sick to his stomach, "And I love you", looking at her with a sexy stare that he knows she likes. "You know Susan; I've been such a fool for not spending time with a woman as beautiful as my wife." Thinking about his Secretary; "I don't know what I would do without you." Thinking about her money, "It really excites me to think about our future, He thinks about the hit man."

"Oh Tyler," "That's so sweet," Susan smiles with tears in her eyes. "You know, if my plan works out the way I expect it to, I will never have to work late ever again." "What did I do to deserve a man as wonderful as you," "Who wants to spend time with me- and will do whatever it takes to make that happen?"

"I'm so lucky to have someone like you." "I Love you!" She says smiling. "I love you too, and from here my love," The only thing that's standing in our way of a beautiful success, is merely a little matter of the process of elimination, that's when true happiness is inevitable" He says smiling deviously.

"I agree," she says, "True happiness will be inevitable." The waiter approaches the table, while taking their order, Tyler's phone beeps indicating a message.

He looks down at his phone to see the message that reads: *I'm here what do you want me to do?"* Tyler tells Susan, "I'm sorry honey I have to respond to this text, its business." "I promise this will be the last interruption of the night." Susan smiles in a playful mood, "It's ok, I don't mind sharing you with your work."

Tyler smiles, "I'm going to hold you to that," as he looks down at his phone returning a text that read: *'Meet me in the men's room and wait for me in one of the stalls, just make sure you're not seen'* "So when I have to work late again, I don't want to hear you complain." "Oh," you won't, I'm going to surprise you." Tyler smiling deviously, "And I- will surprise you!"

After they place their orders, Tyler excuses himself, "Honey, I'm going to wash up for dinner," "I'll be right back." Susan looks at him with dreamy eyes, and says "Hurry back, I'll miss you." Tyler smiles as if to say the same, "Ok."

Entering the men's room, he walks over to the sink patting his hair waiting for the other men to leave the restroom. When the last man leaves he softly whispers, "Are you here?" "Yes, in here." A voice answers back. Tyler follows the voice to the stall that they're in, and enters the stall to join them. Whispering, "Did anyone see you come in here?" "No, I was very careful." Tyler asks, "Did you do what I told you to do?" The voice responds, "of course I did." Tyler asks, "Do you have it on you?" "Absolutely," the voice replies. "Let me see it!" Tyler demands, "beautiful," it's exactly the one I wanted."

"Why do we have to do it here, why couldn't it be somewhere more private?" The voice asks. "If we get caught- "Stop worrying" Tyler interrupts," "We won't get caught," "I need to do this while she's here," "It will make me feel so much better knowing that she was here when it happened." "It would be too obvious to do it at the house."

"Besides it will be too loud at the house." The voice replies, "So then, what are we waiting for?" "Let's do it!" "I thought you'd see it my way!" Tyler pulls Sherri's G-string to the side; the one he told her to being and then takes off her clothes and makes passionate love to her in the stall, while his wife waits for him at the dinner table. Kissing her passionately, he whispers, "You see," "I told you you're my part Two!"

Seattle, Washington

Spirits torment Karen

Karen's previous shocking episode caused her children to keep a close watch on her. Her secret about the fire is starting to attract the underworld. Karen sending hell back to hell in the absence of God, disturbed the underworld who's determined to recruit and destroy her; knowing that the truth could never be told.

"Mama, I'm headed to work, are you going to be ok?" asks Samuel. "Sammie, I'm fine, you go on to work and stop worrying about me so much." "I'm ok- so I wigged out one night, big deal!" "That doesn't mean I'm losing it or crazy; I just had a lot on my mind and I ended up scaring myself somehow." "Really, I'm fine."

"Mama, we know you're not losing it or crazy, but seeing you on the floor shaking like that really gave us a scare and you know Rachael, she's already scared of her own shadow, so you know it freaked her out." "The bottom line mama is that we're both really worried about you, since dad died, you really haven't talked about him at all and that concerns us, knowing how much you two loved each other."

"I know you're hurting, because we're hurting and I don't know about anybody else, but, dad was my mentor." "I didn't just lose a dad, I lost a friend." "I would give anything to have him back, but I know that's not a reality," "So I just deal with it and that's what I'm saying to you mama, stop fighting it and just deal with it." "It's never going to get any better until you learn to deal with it!"

"I'm so sorry, I do know how close you and your father were, and yes, I loved your father very much," "But there's just some things that- you could never understand- and- I- could never tell you." "I love you both so very much and it would kill me to lose you," "So just put up with me for a little while longer," "I promise, I'll- I'll deal with it." Karen says with a faint smile.

Samuel looks at her trying to understand what she means, "Ok mama, take all the time you need," "We'll be right here when you need us," "I love you to mama," "I gotta go to work, I'll see you later, bye." "Ok baby see you soon." He slowly turns and walks out the door.

Karen just stands in the middle of the floor looking at the door when he left. She wants so badly to tell him about the fire, but in her heart she knows he wouldn't understand. While standing there an unexpected spirit appears behind her.

In a raspy soft voice, "How touching, mama's little boy misses his daddy, ha- ha- ha- ha- ha- ha- ha- how sad!" "I can help with that you know," "I can take him up on his- 'do anything to have him back offer." "What do you say, you wanna trade places," the spirit laughs.

Standing frozen stiff, scared to death, Karen stutters, "I- don't know- who you are- or- what you want." "She closes her eyes, "But you need to leave this house and never return!" "Oh come on, you're not playing very nice," "Now why would we leave this house when we just moved in?" "Now that wouldn't be too hospitable of us now, would it?" The spirit asks. Karen is too frightened to move, "What do you mean "we?"

"My God will not allow you to stay in my house, this house is holy, you will leave this house now! "She commands, "Ha- ha- ha- ha- ha- ha- ha- your god!" Ha- ha- ha- ha- ha- how cute, have you seen him lately or heard from him?" "Oh yesssss I almost forgot- you think he authorized your little fire don't you?" The spirits laughs, "I'm so sorry to be the bearer of bad news - "Or Not!" "But he didn't, ha, ha, ha, ha, ha- oops!" "I'm sorry, did I break your trust in your, "Absent god," "Aw, don't worry, we'll take good care of you and your family, ha- ha- ha-ha-ha-ha- We promise!"

Karen begins speaking in the spirit, "I rebuke you in the name of Jesus!" "You will leave this house right now!" The Angel of Mercy stands by her request. The spirit says, "Well-well- "Mercy," "How've you been?" Laughing, "It's been a long time," "I see you're still taking orders from your- "Absent god", laughing "it's all good, "I'll go- Ha, ha, ha, ha, ha- "But I'll be back!" The spirit leaves vanishing into thin air.

Karen, unable to see Mercy protecting her, "Thank you Jesus!" She falls to her knees and cries, as she reflects on the words from the spirit that circled her head.

New Hope, Virginia

Grandma Ames is in her kitchen making breakfast talking to her daughter, "Brenda baby, how do you want your eggs?" Brenda laughs, "Mama I know you didn't just ask me that." "All those seasonings that you put in your food, I would be a fool to try and tell you what to do with it," "but don't you worry, one of these days, my cooking is going to be just as good as yours." Grandma Ames, laughs, "Girl you a mess, I don't know what I'm gonna do with you." Brenda laughs, "Just love me and keep feeding me."

As Grandma Ames reaches for a dish, she falls against the counter as a vision over takes her eyes. She begins to see a bad spirit laughing and she could hear a woman's voice praying to God, but couldn't hear what the woman was saying. Then she sees a bunch of spirits gathered in one place roaming freely and laughing, she sees young people caught in chains trying to get away. The last thing she sees is a weak image of the Angel of Mercy. As the vision leaves her, she becomes weak.

Brenda sees her mother falling, runs over to catch her, "Mama," "What's wrong, are you ok?" "Come on mama sit down, how do you feel, should I call the doctor?"

Grandma Ames sits at the kitchen table holding her head, "I'm ok baby, but somebody's not!" She says. "What do you mean mama, who's not?" Brenda asks "God blessed me with the gift of sight and he just now showed me a woman and her family being attracted by a pool of demons, and her faith is weak," "I got to help her- I got to help her stay strong and fight!" "Otherwise, her soul will be lost."

Brenda stands nervously, starring at her mama, afraid of the journey yet to come with her visions.

Atlanta, Georgia

Tammy and her friend Kiekie meet in the back of Southern General Hospital; Tammy is dressed for her shift, on her day off. "KK, wait right here," "I'm going to check into work," "I'll tell them that I need some over time and it should be no problem." "All right girl hit me on my cell phone, when you need me to come in!" KK replies. Tammy walks up the back stairs way, "Ok cool." Kiekie softly yells out to Tammy, "Hey T, you did remember the needles didn't you?" Tammy Whispers back, "Yeah, I got them in my purse." She quickly runs up the stairs.

Tammy walks into her boss's office, "hello Mr. Stevens." "Tammy," "How are you?" "I'm sorry to hear about your daughter, if there's anything I can do- if you need anything just let me know." He offers.

"There is one thing, I really need some overtime and I know this is my day off, but I can't sit in that house another day without going crazy" she explains."

"Sure!" "Yes, of course just clock in and do what you do and if you need to leave early just let me know, I do understand." Mr Stevens says. "Thank you so much Mr. Stevens." "You're welcome Tammy." "You just take it easy today." "I will sir, thanks again." She leaves his office and goes to the ladies room to make her call to Kiekie.

On the phone, "Hey girl, the coast is clear, I'm in," "He even said I could leave early if I wanted to, that's even better." Kiekie asks, "So what's the plan, how we gonna do it?" "I'm not sure yet, let me find her first and we'll go from there." "All right, just hit me up and let me know when you're ready to move into action." Tammy walks, to the front desk to inquire about the patients. "Hey Carol, hi you doing?" "Hey Tammy, what are you doing here, I thought you had the day off?" "I did, but I needed the overtime, so I came in," "So who we got today, "Anybody new?"

Carol looks at her chart, "Not really, just the one lady on the second floor she- oh wait a minute- that's not right, she's on this floor, she came in a few days ago with a major head injury, she was real close to death at one point; she's still in the intensive of care unit."

"So I guess you're the lucky one who gets to work that unit." "If I were you, I would have just kept my days off, cause that sh#t is a lot of work." Tammy's looking at the chart, "yeah right, whatever," "What room is she in?"Carol glances at her chart again, "uuuuuuh- unit 219."

"Well let me go see what I got myself into," "talk to you later." As Tammy walks down the hall to unit 219, she can hear voices coming from the room. As she prepares to introduce herself as the nurse on board today, she opens the door and sees two men in business suits talking to Regina who's lying in the hospital bed. The men turn to see who entered the room. Barely able to talk, Regina looks over at Tammy and points, "That's her, that's the one who did this to me!"

"Ma'am, we need to speak with you" says one of the men in the suits. Tammy starts to panic, turns and runs as fast as she can down the hall towards the exit door. She hears the detectives on their radio yelling,

"We need some back up on the third floor, suspect is a black female in her late thirties, approximately 5 foot 6 in height about 145 pounds, she's headed North towards the exit. Tammy pushes through the people in the hallway; she knows where they were going to look for her so she detours to the left through a private office, with a private elevator to the parking deck. She calls her friend Kiekie on her cell phone while running towards the parking lot.

She yells, "Hey girl I'm hot, meet me in the parking deck and have the car ready to go, don't ask me any questions just do it!" "I will explain later, c'mon NOW!" As she reaches the parking lot, Kiekie is waiting for her, close to where they met earlier. Tammy jumps in the car and Kiekie hits the accelerator as they speed out of the parking lot.

Busting through the checkout guard arm, they head south taking several back streets. Tammy's constantly looks behind her to make sure she's not being followed.

"Turn left here, don't take the expressway, that's where they're going to look first, hit that side road and go through the back woods, I have a partner who can hide me out for a couple of days; until I can figure out what I'm going to do!" She says to Kiekie whose driving extremely fast.

"What the hell happened in there?" Kiekie shouts! "When I got to her room that bi#@h was talking to two detectives about me, they told me that they needed to speak with me, and I got the hell on!" That bi#@h is dead!" Tammy says angrily!

Kiekie still driving fast, "Don't worry about that right now," "We gotta make sure you're safe," "You leave that bi$#h to me," "I know just who to call, who pretty much runs the motherf#%&in hospital!" "We'll handle this first, and then we'll handle her!" Tammy vows, "She thinks she's hurting now," "She ain't seen nothing yet!"

Brooklyn, New York

Tyrone is at his house sitting on the couch starring at the walls thinking hard about Candy and what she's going through. He decides to call on some of his boys for help. He picks up his cell phone and calls his boy Zach. Zach answers the phone; "Yeah." "Yo Zach, what's up cuz, its T," "hey I need a favor man, can you get in touch wit the crew and meet me at my crib in 30?" Zach asks, "What's going on dog, you all right?" "Naw cuz, I gotta holla at ya'll, bout some serious sh#t, man."

If you can do dat for me cuz, that would be straight!" Tyrone explains. "Oh you know I got cha dog," "I'll holla back in 20 and let cha know what's up." "Cool cuz, dat's what's up, later!"

As Tyrone hangs up the phone, his doorbell rings. He walks over to answer it. "Who is it?" "Its Mike fool, who the hell you think it is?" "I don't know, it could have been the Po-Po." Tyrone says joking. "If dats the case," "Then my next question would be why the fu#k you hiding from the Po-Po?" "Come in fool!" "So what's going on wit cha?" "Nothing yo, just trying to handle some sh#t." "I called Zac and told him to round up the crew, so we can find dat nigga dat caused my baby to suffer like she is!"

Feeling left out, "Oh, so you weren't gonna call me then huh?" "Why I gotta call you when you already here?" "You didn't know I was coming!" "Fool you come here every day!" "Dat's besides da point," "Yo a#s supposed to call a nigga when you trying to round up sum sh#t, Gotd#@nmit!" "I'm a part of the Gotd$#n crew too nigga!" "Naw, but yo a#s gonna call on Zac, some old hard nigga, somebody who wanta f$#k niggas up for fun!"

Tyrone laughs, "Do I detect a little jealousy?" Waving him off with his hand, Mike walks to the refrigerator, "Whatever punk!" "I got your punk cuz." Tyrone's cell phone rings, "yeah what's up?" "All right dog, I got four of our partner's headed yo way so be looking out." "Cool cuz, good looking out." "I told you I got you dog." All right cool, later cuz."

Hollywood, California

Susan is working-out at the gym, when she recognizes an acquaintance at the same gym. She is on the treadmill with her hair in a ponytail and a towel around her neck. After a few minutes, she reaches in her bag and grabs her headphones. While listening to her music, another young lady gets on the treadmill next to hers. Both women were minding their own business, when Susan's treadmill suddenly stops working. "What the hell?" looking at the control panel she begins pushing buttons, trying to get it to resume.

Taking off her headphones and resting them on her shoulder, she looks around for help. She sees the other lady walking on the treadmill beside hers; she reaches over to tap her shoulder inquiring for help. "Excuse me", taping the woman to get her attention, "do you know how to get this treadmill to resume?"

The woman snaps out of her zone, realizes someone was tapping her, looks over to see who it was she realizes she knows the lady. "Susan!" "What are you doing here?" She asks. "Trying to get my treadmill to resume." "Wait, how did you know my name?" "Really," "You don't remember me?" The woman asks. "I'm sorry, you look familiar, but I can't place where I know you from." Being facetious, "And how long have I been working for your husband, Tyler?"

Surprised; Oh my god Sherri!" "Wow!" You look so different, how long has it been since I've last seen you- about a year now?" Sherri responds. "Really," "It's been that long?"

"Oh my goodness, I can't believe I didn't recognize you." "I guess I was just too tied up with this stupid treadmill, it just stopped on me!" "Yeah, that one will do it to you, it's the oldest one they have. I don't know why they haven't done away with it yet!"

Getting off her treadmill, Sherri walks over to Susan's tread mill. "Sometimes you just have to give it a good kick!" She kicks the side of the machine, a few times, causing it to work again. "See," "It works every time." She said Smiling.

"Wow," you really know these machines!" "Well, the truth is, I used to use that one and it stopped on me also, so I kicked it out of anger and it started working again, that's how I knew to kick it!" They both laugh. Sherri asks "So, did you just join here?" "No, I've been coming here for years, what about you?" "I've been a member off and on for the past Five years, but I only come on Tuesday's and Thursday's." Sherri replies.

"I hardly get the chance to work out at all, but since my husband is starting to spend more time with me, I wanted to look my best for him;" Susan says touching her waist and stomach "So that I can still fit in the nice lingerie. She laughs. "Really," Sherri says showing a little jealousy. "Well, I'm sure with the new account he just took over, Tyler won't have much time at all."

"Tyler," "You're on a first name basis now? "Oh- uh- he really hates it when I call him Mr. Chapman, he says it's too- formal," Sherri says trying to make her jealous.

"I see, you said you come here on Tuesday's and Thursday's; today is Wednesday," "So why aren't you at work?" Pushing her hair behind her ear, "Funny you should ask, Tyler had a big meeting today and gave me the day off," "So I thought I'd get a little extra workout." "I mean, I never know when he's going to present me to his business partners," she says laughing, "He always has me doing presentations or something."

With a half-smile, Susan replies, hum- or something!" "So what assignment does he have you on now?" "Well, it's really not- an assignment, I never look at my work as work; because I enjoy working with Tyler so much." There's really nothing he can ask me that I wouldn't do for him."

Getting a little heated; "Really," "I don't think I've ever met anyone who's quite so dedicated to their boss!" "Then obviously you've never worked for Tyler!" Sherri smiles deviously. "No!" Obviously I haven't, although me being his wife and all, I guess that means he works for me!"

Striking back Sherri responds, "I can see how you would see it like that, I mean- I feel the same way when he- well- never mind-it doesn't matter." "I just think he's a great boss and no one- can replace him." Susan pushes the conversation, "No, please- continue- when he what?" Sherri tries to defuse the conversation. "Really Susan, it's just business, nothing personal," "He's too professional for that and besides- you're all he talks about."

"Does he now?" "And what exactly does he say about me?" "Well for starters, he told me about that nice restaurant he took you to.

He said that he enjoyed EVERY moment of it, and that he can't wait for the chance to do it all over again!" Sherri says as she deviously smirks. "He said that no one has ever made him feel like that before- I think he wanted to stay there longer, but she- I mean- they were about to close!"

"Wow," "He told you all that," "What else did you two talk about, being that he's so open with you?" "Oh, it's nothing, you know how men are, they can tell everyone else how they feel except the ones they're with." She said changing the mood.

Letting her guard down, "Yeah, I guess you're right about that, because until that night, I never really knew how much he loves me and really wants to be with me." "Oh trust me, when I say you are his major focus, in more ways than one."

Changing the subject, "You know- I've already said- way too much, Tyler would kill me if he knew I told you his feelings." Susan smiles, "well don't worry, your secret is safe with me." Sherri changes the subject. "Are you hungry?" "Do you wanta get something to eat?" "Yeah, I guess I've worked up an appetite between walking on this tread mill and trying to get it to work; so yeah let's get something to eat."

They walk out of the gym talking and laughing. They decide to go to a small, back alley restaurant that Sherri suggested. Sherri mentions the delicious food they serve there. Susan is very relaxed being with Sherri. So relaxed, that they both ride together in Susan's car at Sherri's request.

45mins later they arrive at what looked to be an abandoned area on the rough side of town. Susan becomes a little nervous of the area. "Are you sure we're in the right place, this looks a bit deserted" She says looking around. "Well, you know some of the best food comes from the not so popular areas" Sherri says trying to calm her down.

"You're right, maybe I just need to get out more." "I'm so used to the upper class neighborhoods that I can't appreciate much else!" They pull up to an old abandoned building with an old, worn out sign that's barely hanging. That read, Moe's Restaurant. "Here we are- "Oh no!" "It can't be!" "Are you serious?"

"I was just here last week!" Something isn't right about this, wait here!" Sherri gets out of the car and walks between two narrow, brick walls. About an hour goes by and Sherri hasn't returned. Susan is beginning to worry about Sherri's safety; she gets out of her car to look for her. Afraid of what happens after dark on that side of town.

"SHERRI!"- "SHERRI!" Where are you?" Starting to panic as the sun is beginning to go down. Not wanting to leave without Sherri, she gets out of the car and follows the path Sherri took between the buildings. "SHERRI!" "Where are you?

The area is dark, with very dim lights near the window areas. It's an old warehouse with slabs of broken concrete and large columns of concrete pillars that reach the tall ceiling throughout the building. Susan continues walking through the huge and scary, warehouse calling for Sherri.

She trips on a slab of concrete and falls into a sewer puddle, cutting her leg badly. She can no longer see the entrance of the building. She slid her body to one of the big pillars and pulls herself up from the floor. "SHERRI!" da#mit, where are you?" She yells. "Sherri- I need your help!"

No response, Just silence. Susan thinks something may have happened to Sherri; she started limping back towards the way she came in. It's quickly getting darker by the minute; it's too dark to see anything. With tears in her eyes, she stumbles over everything.

She begins to hear footsteps moving towards her, but can't see who it is. "Sherri!" "Is that you, Sherri?" No answer. Susan turns towards the sound of the footsteps, and calls out to Sherri again. She then hears an extremely loud sound that echoes off the walls. Suddenly she feels an impact to her leg that causes an extreme burning sensation, causing her leg to give out and she falls, hitting her head on the concrete. She lays there unconscious.

"Is she dead?" Sherri asks. A man's voice says, "You didn't have to shoot her!" "Let me see." He reaches down to check her pulse. "No," but she hit her head pretty hard." "Let's get her out of here, and into the back room, we'll stitch her up and make sure she's comfortable."

Sherri says angrily, "What difference does it make if she's comfortable or not let's just get rid of her!" "It makes a lot of difference; we can't hold a dead or half dead person hostage. So shut the f#@k up and just do what I tell you to do!" "You've done great up to this point, don't ruin it now!" "I'm sorry, I'm not trying to ruin anything, I just want her out of our way." "And so do I, but we have to be smart about it, because a lot of money is riding on this!"

"That's my reason for not hiring a hitman; I didn't need any loose ends." "It's just you and me now, and the only thing standing between us, is this matter of the process of elimination!" "And when it's all said and done, no more loose ends!" "Only then will true happiness be inevitable!" Tyler says smiling.

"So what now?" "Like I said, we take care of her, making sure she's ok." "Then we lock her up down here." "When she wakes up, she'll have one hell of a headache, but she'll be worth billions!" "Billions that dear ole daddy will be willing to die for!"

Seattle, Washington

Samuel, Karen's son, is at work when one of his co-worker's named Dianne, is determined to break his spiritual walk with God. Dianne is, a strange girl, in her late thirties who's been working on the job for 6 years. She always wears black clothes, black painted nails, black hair and black lipstick. No one really bothers her, because strange things were known to happen around her. All of a sudden, she inquires about Julie, after many years of talking to no one.

"Hey girl, what you got going on after work today?" Dianne asks Julie. "I don't know". "What I really want to do can't be done, so I guess I'll improvise." She says glaring at Samuel. "What is it that you really want to do?" Julie laughs, and says "Samuel!"

113

"Girl, that square, He couldn't get it up if you paid him too!" Dianne jokes. "My point exactly, girl I think he's a virgin." "I've always wanted me a virgin; so I can turn him out." "He's so into the church, I'll bet he doesn't even go to the movies." Julie says frowning.

"You really want him?" "What I want, and what I'm going to get are two different things." She laughs. "No really, I could get him for you, do you want him?" Dianne asks again. "Absolutely" "Ok, consider it done!" Dianne says looking at Samuel with a half-smile. "How do you pose to do that?" Julie asks concerned.

"Just leave the details to me, you'll have him by 9pm tonight at your house, alone" Dianne says confidently. Laughing, Julie is not buying it. "I know you're dreaming now, there's no way he's coming to my house especially at that time of night!" Dianne replies, "If I do this for you, you'll owe me some day!" "Owe you what?" Dianne smiles, "you'll see when the time comes!"

Samuel walks into the break room to get a cup of coffee, and Dianne walks in behind him. "Hi Sammy, how's it going?" Dianne asks. Only his mother calls him Sammy. He looks around to see who called him Sammy. Dianne smiles deviously, "You mind buying me a coffee too?"

Trying to be sociable, "Sure, why not." Placing his cup of coffee on the table, he turns around to the coffee machine to get her coffee. Dianne reaches over and puts her finger in his coffee and stirs it around whispering some words to herself, she pulls her finger out and slowly licks the coffee from her finger. Samuel turns back around and hands her the coffee he brought for her.

Dianne holds up her cup of coffee as if to make a toast, "here's to a very nice guy." She says smiling. Not really wanting to talk, Samuel decides to entertain her by doing the toast. They clicked their paper cups together and sipped their coffee; Samuel hoping she'll go away. "Ok, so, back to work", he says walking pass her.

Back at his desk, Samuel starts to feel a little weird, but thinks it's because he's tired.

Dianne walks back to her chair beside Julie and whispers to her. "Ok, it's done, I saw Sammy in the break room and I told him that you were crazy about him, he asked me "Why you couldn't tell me this herself"?

Very excited," "For real- don't play with me Dianne." "Why would he want me to talk to him, he's never even acknowledged that I'm alive." "Are you going to talk to him or what?" "What am I supposed to say to him?" "Try asking him out to dinner at your house tonight, at 9." Unsure, "Wow!" "Are you sure about this?" Dianne encourages her, "You better hurry before he gets ready to leave!"

Julie nervously walks two aisles over to Samuel's desk. As she approaches his desk, he looks up at her. "Can I help you?" Nervously, she hesitates with a half- smile, "I- I- I was- wondering- if you wanted to- uh- have dinner- with me- tonight?" Unexpectedly, Samuel surprises her, "Sure, why not!" Nearly passing out. "REALLY" I mean great- uh my house- uh at 9?" Samuel tries to say no, but says, "I'll be there!"

Julie walks back to her desk in shock. "What in the hell did you say to him," He's so- so- easy?" She asks Dianne. "I didn't say anything to him; I just thought in my head what he should say to you." "I can't believe he just said yeah!" What are the odds?" Oh- Oh My Gosh I can't cook, what am I going to do?"

"Who said anything about cooking, just get him there and pretend to order out, and while waiting for the delivery, do what you've always wanted to do!" I Mean, What man goes to a woman's house that time of night unless he's after something?" "Yeah, I never thought about it like that." "Should I tell him where I live?" Smiling deviously, "Don't worry about that, I'll make sure he finds his way."

"How do you know where I live?" "You've never been to my house." Smiling deviously, "There's a lot of things I know about you." Looking curiously, "like what?" Dianne thinks how to say it, "For one thing, you have no faith, which makes it's easy for me to know you." She laughs, and then changes the subject, "But that's for another time." "Right now, let's get you hooked up."

Julie snaps out of her brief daze, "Oh yeah, hooked up, right." "Thank you so much, I so owe you." Dianne smiles and then laughs, "More than you realize!"

The choices of mankind in the absence of God, has become more than unbearable. Without God, pain and suffering has no end. Who then will bear the burdens for mankind as they lean upon their own understanding? Distorted paths lead to massive destructions that inevitably unleash the underworld to freely roam the earth, before their appointed time.

New Hope, Virginia

Grandma Ames and her daughter are in church, God reveals Samuel's destruction to Grandma Ames. Since the absence of God, only about ten people are in the congregation.

Many members of the church have left, after realizing that their true dedication was never to God, but to the world.

Among the ten members are two men, the Bishop, a highly anointed man of God; and his Co-Pastor, who is a man after God's heart. Seven of the members were elderly women who are known as the highly anointed prayer intercessors of the church, and then Brenda the tenth member, who faithfully holds to her belief in God.

"Gather around Saints, we need to pray for God's people, pray that they will be able to withstand these evil days." says The Bishop. As the people gathered in a circle to pray, they all hold hands. Momma Ames begins to shake rapidly while connected to the circle. The anointing was so strong at that moment that everyone in the circle begins to see the visions given to Momma Ames.

They begin to see the devil dressed in black, in a work place, seeking whomever he can devour, they see him dragging chains. They can see a young man fighting for his life but is being over taken by the evil placed upon him.

Bishop tells everyone, "Pray Saints- pray- we need to stop Satan in his tracks and bring down his strong hold against that young man. Pray like it's your own child." Everybody begins to pray intensely and the Angels of God were compelled to move on their behalf.

Seattle, Washington

Samuel drives to Julie's house, with a clear knowledge of the directions. Arriving at her house, he gets out of his car slightly confused. He walks to her door and rings the bell at exactly 9pm. Samuels' struggling with a force that makes him want to be there and a force that makes him want to leave.

Julie does her last minute preparations, "Just a minute, I'll be right there." She walks to the door, opening it to greet Samuel, "Hi, wow, you are quite the prompt person aren't you?" "Come in." "Would you like something to drink?" She asks politely.

Samuel is confused, "Um- no I-I'm fine, what are we doing here?" "Why did you all of a sudden want me to have dinner with you?" He asks. She Half-smiles, "Well, it wasn't really all of a sudden, I mean, I have always liked you and wanted to go out with you, but I was too afraid to ask.", "So than why now?" Samuel asked, "Where did this sudden boldness come from?"

Julie searches for an answer, "I was told that you wanted me to ask you out." He frowns. "You were told that by whom?" Julie doesn't know how to say it, "Uh- By- by Dianne; she said that she told you about me wanting to talk to you, and that, you asked her why I couldn't tell you that myself."

Starting to get upset, "I never said anything to Dianne about you, and further more- He stops instantly, because of a sudden bad headache. "Uuhhh!" As he holds his head in pain, Julie looks at Samuel concerned. "Are you ok, come on, sit down, what is it, what's wrong?"

Samuel replies, "I'm not sure, I just got this bad headache all of a sudden." Panicking, Julie asks, "Do you want me to get you something, an aspirin or some water or something?" Samuel, holding his head, "No just- give me a moment." Julie sits there nervously looking at him wanting to help. "Are you sure, I can't get you anything?" She offers. His headache slowly starts to subside. "It's going away now." Julie smiles, "I'm glad, you gave me quite a scare."

Samuel takes his hands from his head, "I apologize, I never meant to scare you, whew!" "That was some headache, that's never happened to me before, I don't know what happened."

Julie calms down, "I'm just glad you're ok, I didn't know what to do." "So, now what, what do you want to do?" "I know I was supposed to have cooked dinner, but the truth is, I can't cook." Samuel lets out a slight laugh. "It's ok, I wasn't hungry anyway. You're a very sweet young lady; I don't know how I managed to miss you at work."

She leans back on the couch, and smiles. "You were always so wrapped up in your work or church, that you didn't have time to notice much else, that alone- me." Feeling a little sad, "I'm so sorry, I never meant to be so distant; I guess I just have a lot on my plate lately, with my mother and all."

"If you don't mind me asking, what's wrong with your mother?" Samuel leans back on the coach with one hand on his forehead. Uhh- I don't know, she just lost my father in a church fire not too long ago, and ever since then she's been acting so strange, I mean, she claims that, she sees him from time to time, I don't know whether to believe her or commit her at times."

"I can see how you would have a lot on your mind." "So, what are you going to do, is she ok, does she need help, what do you think she needs?" Shaking his head, "I don't know, I just want her to deal with my dad's death and move on." "I feel she's holding on to something that's trying to drive her insane, and I refuse to let that happen."

Julie smiles, "I was right about you, you're a good man. "There are not many guys out there who cares about helping their mom get over things." "She's lucky to have a son like you."

Samuel stares at Julie. "Yeah well, I'm lucky to be able to spend time with someone like you." As he slowly grabs her hands and looks her in the eyes.

"How would you like to have dinner with me tomorrow night, at a nice restaurant where you don't have to cook; and at a decent time." "A quiet place; where we could really enjoy each other's company in a slightly different atmosphere." He suggests.

She's excited about him asking her out for real this time. "I would absolutely love too!" Samuel smiles, "Great, I would really like that." He stands up gently pulling her up by her hands respectfully. "I must go now, as he looks into her eyes smiling, "In a weird sort of way, I actually enjoyed this time with you and look forward to seeing you again." He kisses her on the forehead and gives her a hug. Julie hugs him back, "Me too- in a- weird sort of way." They both laugh.

Julie walks Samuel to the door and waves goodbye as he walks to his car and then closes the door behind her. With her back against the door she, leans her head back and closes her eyes. She takes a long breath and says, "So not what I expected," she smiles, "But I like it."

New Hope, Virginia

The prayers of the righteous availed much. Everyone in the prayer circle begins thanking God and dancing for joy, when the Angels revealed the outcome of the chains being broken from the young man, as what was meant for evil was turned into good. The breaking of the chains caused a sharp pain to flow through Samuel's head, but in the end, it made him free.

Brooklyn, New York

Tyrone and Mike are sitting on the couch drinking and talking. The doorbell rings, it's the four guys Zach sent. Tyrone walks over to the door peeping through the peep hole, "Who is it?" "It's yo boys G!" Tyrone opens the door, "Yeah, what's up cuz?" giving them a firm handshake and hug. "Thanks for coming through y'all." Chris is the quiet one of the group, "its' all good G, dat's wut we spose to do for our peps cuz."

Bobby, the Trigger man, "So what's up, what you got going on?" The pessimistic one is known as Flare, "dis can't be good!" He says. Stretch, the optimistic one of the group;

"C'mon G, ain't noting dat bad." Zach, known as the soulless one, "Whatever it is we can handle it!"

Tyrone tells everyone to come in and makes themselves at home. "Ya'll remember Mike right?" as he looks at Mike. "Yeah we remember Mike, your side kick." "Ain't nothing wrong with dat, we all need one of those." says Bobby.

Mike checks him, "One of what, fool?" "I ain't no gotd#@n dog motherfu$#er!" Bobby clarifies the situation, "ain't nobody said you were a gotd@#n dog nigga," "I was given you compliment Bi%ch," Mike replies, "I got cho Bi%ch" nigga! Bobby ignores him, "man whatever, ANYWAY, what's going on T, your Rover over there, needs a bone." Mike gives Bobby the finger, "bone dis bi#@h!" Tyrone breaks it up, "all right, aright, come on y'all we got some serious sh#t to discuss." "Y'all heard about my girl Candy right?"

Trying to remember, Zach says, "Candy-Candy- dat name sounds familiar." Bobby says, "That's the chick wit da crazy moms right?" Tyrone agrees, "yeah, yeah dat's da one." Bobby says, "dat Mother$#@er almost got her a@s shot; She came running up on me and my boys talking about 'leave my g#@@#%n daughter alone and stay da f#@k

124

away from her!" "I was like b$#@h you need to back the hell up, I don't even know who the f#@k yo daughter is bi$%h!"

Flare inquires, "Where was I when dat happened?" "I don't know, but you wasn't wit us", Bobby says. "Dat sounds like something dat "Bi%#h" would say, She told me and Mike to get the f$#k off her porch and it was Candy's house!" Tyrone says.

"I didn't know what the hell she was talking about, I almost put a cap in her a#s!" Bobby says. Chris, Busting out in laughter, "I remember dat sh@t man, it took about three of us to get yo gun out of yo hand; that sh@t was funny as hell!"
Everybody's laughing with Chris. "Man you crazy!" "Anyway, Candy's in the crazy house because some fool put a bullet in her old man's head, while she was pregnant with his kid. By the time I met her she had already lost it because of dat sh@t!" "What da f$#k does dat have to do with you?" Zach asked.

"I guess you missed the part I said about her being my girl," "that's what the f#@k it has to do with me!" "Talk to me dog, Zach says, cus you were starting to sound like you were trying to revenge her old man's killer or something." Tyrone says seriously, "I am, but not for the reasons that you're thinking about." "Dat girl is my heart man, and to see her suffering like dat, just drives me crazy!"

"All she wants to know is who did it, and dat's what I gotta do, I gotta find dat nigga that caused her dis pain; so that my baby can be at peace!" "Cuz, you don't know what it's like to see da woman dat you love cry in her sleep-thinning out because she can't eat. It's not about him Cuz, it's about bringing closure to dis sh#t so dat me and my girl can be good again!"

"You a bigger man, than I am G, cause I would have just let that b#@%h deal with dat sh@t" herself, and told her to call when the fu&k' she got over it!" "But you my boy, so if dat's what you wanta do, then dat's what we gonna do!" "Just tell me how you want us to handle dis sh*t and we got you."

Tyrone thanks them. "This really means a lot to me cuz." "She said dat he called out some nigga's name before he died." "We need to find out who it was he told it to; so we can find out who it was and whatever name comes up, we gonna search every Joe blow wit dat name until we find da fool who smoked her old man!" Zach agrees, "Consider it done!" Bobby Holding his gun up. "Yeah cause I'm gonna be da one to smoke dat b#@*h!" "Whoever it is, his time is up!" says Tyrone.

Atlanta, Georgia

Kiekie and Tammy pull off the main city streets and onto a dirt road that leads to an old brick house with a large barn in the back of the house. "Right there, there it is, those mother$#@er's will never find me here!", Tammy says.

"Who the hell lives here", Kiekie asks? "Larry, he's an old fling of mine, he's lived here forever and a day. Stay here, I'm going to see if he's home." Tammy walks up the dirt road to her friend Larry's house. She knocks on the door four times. Looking through the glass window beside the door, she sees Larry coming. "Who is it?", Larry asks. "It's me Larry, Tammy." "Tammy who," Larry asks. "What the hell do you mean Tammy who, how many Tammy's do you know?" She says sternly. Larry opens the door, "Oh it's you, I didn't know who you were."

"Oh, so it's like that?" Tammy says. "Well hell, I only hear from you when you need something, what do you expect, I haven't heard from you in about three years." "Now you know you're telling one Larry, it hasn't been that long." "Well hell, its pretty da#n close, what you doing here for anyway?" "Well d#@n is that the hello I get?" "Well pardon me, hello! "Now what the hell do you want? "Look I kind of got myself in a little jam, and I need your help." Tammy explains. "What kind of jam, I ain't got no money!"

"I don't need no money Larry, I need a place to lay low until I can figure out what I'm going to do." "What you mean lay low?" "Figure out what you gonna do about what?"

I'm in a little trouble Larry, I was trying to revenge my daughter's death, and I- look, can I say here for a couple of days or what?" Larry asks, "What the hell are you talking about; revenge your daughter's death?" "What the hell is wrong wit yo daughter?" And who the hell did you try to revenge?"

"Look, can I come in; it's really not a good idea for me to be standing out here in the open." Tammy says. "Aw hell," What kind of sh@t is this?" "You got the man on you?" "Hell Naw, you can't lay low here, I ain't no gotd@%*n hide-out." "You need to take dat s#@t somewhere else, cause I ain't the one." "I don't need no trouble with the man"

"Larry please" I don't know what else to do, I can't go to jail. Just let me stay here for a couple of days, and till this blows over, and then I can get out of town," Tammy begs.

"You should've thought about that sh@t' before you tried to do whatever it was dat you did. Now what part of the Hell No didn't you understand, the Hell or the No?" "I ain't going to have no parts of this sh#t. You got yo self in dis s#@t, now you can get yourself out of it, Good-bye! Larry tries to close the door but Tammy holds it open with her hand. "Larry wait," You don't understand, you won't be a part of anything.

They don't even know who you are, or where I'm at, they will never think to even look here if they can't connect you to me!" she says.

"I know they won't think to look here, cause you ain't going to be here, and the only connecting that there's going to be, is me connecting to the operator, if you don't get the hell off my property. Now GOOD-BYE!"

He slams the door in her face. Tammy walks back to the car crying. "What is it, what's going on?" Kiekie asks. Tammy leans up against the passenger's door with her head laid back against the top of the car, and then slides her body down to the ground, crying with her head to her knees and her arms around her folded legs.

Kiekie gets out the car and rushes over to Tammy. "What the hell is going on, what did he say, is he going to help us or what?" She asks. Tammy shakes her head, still crying. "No!" She cries, "He said that he didn't want

129

anything to do with me." Sobbing, "What am I going to do Kiekie?" "I can't keep running, I don't even know who I am anymore!" as she continues cries, "What am I going to do now?"

"Sh%t, this sh%t is fu#k*d up. You mean to tell me that that old f$#ker wouldn't even help you?" "What kind of friend is that motherfu%er supposed to be?" Holding her head; "Ok-ok, let's think this thing through."

"We can't go back to your place because that's the first place they'll look, and we can't go back to mine, because they will eventually hook me to you, since I'm sure they got my plates on camera, when we busted through the f#@%ing guard gate!" "What about your brother, do you think he will help us?"

Tammy looks at her frowning, "No!" "If Robert had ANY idea about what I tried to do, he'll never forgive me, no, we have to find somebody else, not Robert." "I hate to break it to you sweetie, but I'm almost sure we're all across the news by now, and if he doesn't know by now, it's just a matter of time before he finds out."

Tammy holds her head crying, "Oh my god, what have I done, what have I done?" Kiekie stands there speechless and crying. "Fu%k, it wasn't supposed to happen like this." They both stand around crying, without the slightest idea of their next move.

Hollywood, California

Susan wakes up on the floor of in an abandoned brick room. Her head throbs with pain and she can't move her leg. Susan screams out, "Help me!" SOMEBODY PLEEESE, HELP ME!" Hhh-hhh- IS THERE ANYBODY OUT THERE, PLEEEESE HELP ME! Hhhhhhh-WHERE AM I!" HELP ME PLEASE!"

Susan tries to move her leg, "ouch, Uh-uh-WHAT DO YOU WANT WITH ME!" WHO DID THIS TO ME, She screams, "WHAT'S HAPPENING?"

Back in the city, Susan's father has a surprised visit from his Son-in-law Tyler. Gary's Secretary calls him on his speaker phone, "Mr. Chandler Sir, you have a visitor in the lobby." "Who is it Beth?" Gary asks. "It's your Son-In-Law Sir." Surprised, "REALLY," Yes, yes, tell him to come in."

Tyler walks into Gary's office, "Gary, it's been awhile." "So what do I owe this surprise visit, Gary asks. "Tyler smiles deviously, "oh, not much, just your life," laughing, I'm just kidding." "Well you don't ask for much do you?" Gary chuckles. Tyler pretends to look concerned, "No, really, I'm here because I'm a little concerned about your daughter. She hasn't been home in a couple of days and I was just wondering if she might have come to you?"

"No, no, she didn't come here. What happened, did you two have a fight or something?" Gary asks. "No! Of course not, we had just made plans to spend more time together, I mean, it was just a week ago I had Sherri send a couple dozen roses to the house for her. I thought we were doing fine." Tyler explains.

"Well, it's not like my Susan to just disappear." "Something had to happen", Gary says. "My sentiments exactly, something HAD to happen." Tyler says. "Have you contacted the police yet," asks Gary. "No, I didn't want to alarm anyone just in case she showed up." Tyler says. "Well, what do you think happened to her, she's ok right?" Gary asks.

"Gary, your guess is as good as mine, I'm worried about her too, I was thinking that we should silently put up some reward money just in case this was a kidnapping situation or something." Tyler explains. "Why would somebody want to kidnap her, who would do something like that?" Gary asks.

Tyler looking very serious, "Gary you failed to realize who you are, everybody knows about your fortune from the tracks, I mean, you're the man." Gary tired of Tyler's BullS%#t, "What the hell are you up too, and where the hell is my daughter?"

Stunned, "Gary, how should I know, I told you she hasn't been home in a couple of days, that's why I came to you." In a rage, Gary yells, "Cut the bull#@$t Tyler, if anything happens to my daughter, I'm coming straight to you." "I know you and that little whore secretary of yours are up to something."

But let's be quite clear about something, I did a little checking too and that anonymous mystery man who your little b#@$h gathered her information about me from," "Works for me." "You really need to watch who you get to handle your dirty work, because not only did she brag to him about her new office with a view; that she's acquiring from her loving boss, she unknowingly, left names and mission statements concerning my death."

Gary continues, "so Tyler, unless you're planning to spend the rest of your miserable f$#@ing life behind bars, without further due, I expect to see my daughter home bright and early in the morning, in the best of f%$#ing health!"

"Now, I really don't think there's a whole hell of a lot more to say about this, do you? You have yourself a good day now Tyler; you're going to need one." With nothing left to be said, Tyler disgustedly walks out of Gary's office.

Seattle, Washington

Karen's in the kitchen fixing lunch, when three of the women from her previous church came to visit her. The doorbell rings. Karen walks over to answer the door. "Sister Palmer, its Mary Collins and some of the sisters here to spend some time with you." Karen opens the door. "Well hello ladies, what a pleasant surprise to see you all. Do come in, make yourselves at home. How have you all been doing?"

"Oh we've been just fine." "How have you been, I have been so worried about you, we all have." "How are you holding up, I know it's been hard for you losing Pastor and all?" Karen walks over to sit on the couch, "Well, I've been as good as to be expected. I mean, I have my moments, but through it all, God has been good to me."

"I guess we've all had our moment that's why we wanted to come by and spend a little time with you, it's been so long since we've had the chance to sit down and talk. We've been praying for you and your family." "To us you will always be our First Lady."

Half smiling, "that's really sweet of you to say, however as of lately, I haven't been feeling much like a First Lady. To be quite honest, I don't know how I feel at times. Sometimes I think I'm losing my mind." Karen says,

"I'm starting to see things that are not there and I'm hearing all sorts of voices from time to time. I don't know what's going on with me these days."

"That seems quite normal to me, I mean, you just lost your husband of many years, and you can't expect that to go away overnight." "The enemy wants you to think that you're losing your mind, but like the word of God says," "The devil comes to steal, kill and destroy, but the devil is a liar, we bind that spirit of defeat in Jesus name." Sister Sonia says. "Sister Karen can we pray with you."

Karen stands up, "oh yes, by all means." The women gather around Karen and began praying for her. "Heavenly father, we thank you for our sister Karen today God and we ask your shield of Mercy to be camped around her, we pray for strength Lord Jesus, we ask that you strengthen her in her hour of weakness, give her peace God, peace that passes all understanding."

"We ask you to build a camp around her O God, and let no weapon formed against her prosper." "We pray that the gates of hell will not prevail, and we bind the hands of the enemy formed against her mind O God." "We declare war against the devil O God, in the name of Jesus; we come against everything that's not of you O God."

"We claim the Victory over the devil O God; we declare it in the name of Jesus." "We break every strong hold against our sister Karen O God." "For Lord you said in your word, that where there are two or three gathered together, you will be in the midst O God, we thank you for your Grace and your Mercy O God, we thank you for your Peace O God, we thank you for being the Lord of Our lives O God, we thank you for all that you've done and all that you are about to do O God." "We love you O God, we Glorify your name O God, for Lord we recognize that there is no greater name than the name of Jesus O God, and we're here to give you all the Glory and all the Honor and all the Praise in that Mighty and Majestic name of Jesus Christ we pray amen and amen."

"Sister Karen, as I was praying for you, The Holy Spirit revealed to me that you are under the attack of the enemy, and that he desires to have you and sift you as wheat. The Lord said that he has placed a Gatekeeper to Guard your soul. He said that this attack that you are under is like nothing that you've ever experienced before; he said that hell is revengeful against you. He said to tell you to waiver not, for if you should fall, there will be no return." She began speaking in other tongues.

The devil was afraid of Sister Sonia, because he knows that she's a seer. Unaware of whom it was revealing his plan against her; he keeps his distance until the women left Karen's home. The prayer of the righteous availed much, and Heaven was touched. God turned his head in the direction of his people for just a moment, long enough to warn Karen.

Heaven

Gabriel says to God, "Lord if I may speak, it is your servant. My Lord, have not mankind suffered long enough without Grace and Mercy, for even the Righteous are under attack. How much longer will you turn your face against mankind." For there stands no chance of survival without you," "Hell has opened to earth in your absence, roaming before their time. Release me my Lord to fight against Hell, for mankind's sake, that I may unleash a fair chance to survival."

God responds to Gabriel's' plea, "Your Love for mankind is as of that of my own, upon their surrendering of hearts will I return unto mankind. Many shall suffer for the hatred of their wicked hearts, while those of faith shall suffer for just a little while, soon I will return unto them and only them. Until this time in which I speak, they shall continue to follow the true desires of their own hearts. They shall without my image see themselves clearly, then and only then will I return for my people who chose me."

New Hope, Virginia

Grandma Ames is on her knees praying when God appears to her in the spirit. "Ames!" Ames!" Says the spirit of God, *Your faith is pleasing to me, for I the Lord thy God have seen thy works and the purity of thy heart. For many shall rise up against you; but I shall deliver you. As far as the east is from the west, there you must go.*

For I the Lord thy God will position you in the path of the righteous for my name sake. There you shall fight the good fight of faith and I will be with you. Seek and you shall find pure faith ordained for your journey, you will know them by their willingness to obey. I the Lord thy God have spoken, and so shall it be."

Grandma Ames, says obediently, "yes Lord for your servant hearth and shall obey."

Brooklyn, New York

The Search

Tyrone's boys left his house around 10pm. Mike and Tyrone are in the house talking after their departure. "Man, this sh#t is finally about to go down cuz!" Tyrone says. "I still don't see why you had to call all those punk a#$ nigga's for some sn#t that we could've handled ourselves!" Mike says upset.

"I don't know what your beef is wit my boys; but you need to swash dat sh#t cuz!" "I mean, we don't know what's up with ole boys killer, he could have some mad protection around him or some sh#t, it's better to be safe than sorry!"

"Not to mention, Zac know people cuz, I mean, he can definitely make some sh#t happen." "I still ain't feeling you dog, I know Zac is yo boy and all, but dat nigga's crazy. That fool can cut a nigga's heart out and eat it and won't give a s#@t about it." "And yo boy Bobby, I can't stand dat motherf#@*er, all dat fool wanna do is shoot somebody. I don't know T, but someum just ain't right about all dis sh#t; I just can't put my finger on it!" Mike wonders.

"Cuz you just paranoid, the only thing ain't right about dis sh#t is dat my baby ain't here wit me because of dat nigga!" "Who knows, dat might be a good thang, in the state of mind she's in she might think you dat nigga and shoot you herself." Mike replies, "Dat's why I gotta find dat nigga, so she can stop seeing him!" Tyrone explains.

"Let me ask you something, I'm just curious. Let's say you find dat nigga who shot ol boy and let's say you got em on the ground wit yo fist drew back getting ready to deck em, in that moment dat you look em in his eyes, who is it really about?" Revenge for yo girl or smoking a nigga dat you ain't got no beef wit, just for the hell of it. Cause the way I see it, it's like you just became obsessed with finding a nigga who ain't did sh#t to you, for somebody who don't even give a f*&k about you!"

Tyrone sits in deep thought about the things Mike said. Speechless, he gets up and walks into his bedroom and closes the door. Mike slowly grabs his jacket and walks out of his house and goes home.

Atlanta, Georgia

Kiekie and Tammy are in the driveway of Larry's house trying to figure out their next plan. "We need to ditch my car, because I'm sure they have my plates on broadcast by now", Kiekie says. "Then what the hell are we supposed to do without a car", Tammy asks? "Look, I know you don't want to involve your brother, but face it, we are sh$t out of options here, you know?"

"There's got to be somebody else; what about some of the people who came to my daughter's funeral reception, somebody has to be willing to help us!" Tammy thinks. "I think you lost face with them when you beat ole girl up in front of them." "What the hell", "We might as well steal a car!" Kiekie advises. "Yeah right, and get grand theft charges added to attempted murder charges, that's a plan!" Tammy says sarcastically. "Well hell, I don't hear you coming up with any brilliant ideas!"

Tammy's cell phone rings. "Who the f#@k is that?" Kiekie says, Tammy looks at her phone,

"Sh#t!" "it's Robert." "Well sh#t, answer it, don't just let it ring. "Hello", "Tammy, are you alright", Robert asks? "Yeah, I'm ok." "What the hell is going on, you're all over the news, on every channel. What the hell did you do?"

"I found out that Regina was admitted into the hospital where I work and I tried to kill her, but she was talking to some detectives when I walked in, they tried to talk to me, but I ran, now here we are!"

"My god Tammy, why didn't you just talk to them, you could have gotten away with insanity or something." "I mean her son did cause your daughter's death. You could have just told them that and went to counseling at the worst." Says Robert, "I'm sorry, I wasn't thinking, the only thing I could think about was going to jail for trying to kill her; but now, it's too late, I've made such a mess of everything, I just don't know what to do now!" Tammy confesses.

"Tammy- Tammy- Tammy, it's not too late, Regina isn't dead, and no crime has been committed, all you have to do is turn yourself in and you can still get away with insanity; but the longer you stay out there and if Regina dies, then it turns into Murder one, and you become a fugitive.

It's not worth it sweetheart. This isn't the way to handle Rhonda's death; this isn't something she would have expected from her mother. Tell me where you are, and I will come and get you, and I'll go with you to turn yourself in. I will do everything in my power to clear your name. I will be there for you Sis; you just have to trust me." Robert explains.

Tammy thinks long and hard about the things her brother said. "You're right. Since I've lost Rhonda, I don't have anything else left to lose. My baby's gone, and I can't bring her back.

I'm on the corner of 6th and 24 off the dirt road; I'll see you when you get here." "Tammy, I'm proud of you. I'm on my way." "So is he coming to get us, Kiekie asks, what's the plan?" Tammy looks at her friend Kiekie with tears in her eyes, "There is no plan, Robert's on his way to get me, so I can turn myself in." "What the- are you sure you want to do this, you're talking about some serious time!" "Look we can take my car and hit the back roads all the way out of this f#%&in state, start all over somewhere else!"

"I know you just want to help me Kiekie, but Robert's right, this isn't something that Rhonda would expect from her mother; Kiekie- hhh- she was all I had, my reason for living, I can't do this, I'm not a killer, I'm not

143

a-bad person-I just- want my baby back. And since that can't happen, it really doesn't matter what they do with me, because the worst has already been done!" Tammy cries.

Kiekie hugs her and cries with her. "I will always be here for you no matter what, and where ever they take you, I'll be there." and for the record- she sobs, you do have another reason to live because I need you and so does Robert. So just know, we love you, she says sobbing, and we'll always have your back."

As they stand hugging each other and crying, Robert pulls in the driveway. Robert gets out of the car and stands there while Kiekie and Tammy say their good- byes. He walks over to Tammy and gives her a hug. "Tammy, I'm so sorry that you had to go through all of this. I love you so much."

"I couldn't even be mad at you, because part of me wanted you to get revenge for her death; but then I realized that it just wasn't right. That's not the way to handle it."

Slowly pulling back from her he holds her face in his hands and looks deeply in her eyes. "You don't have to worry about any- thing; I will never let anything happen to you. We're going to make it through this and if I have to move to Georgia, I'll never leave you alone again.

I love you Tammy you're my baby sister, I should've been here for you- I'm- so sorry, and I will make this right. Robert hugs her again. Tammy turns to look at Kiekie with tears in her eyes. "We would have made a great team." "Not would've, Kiekie says crying, we are a great team. I love you Tammy." "I love you too Kiekie, good-bye."

Tammy turns back around into Robert's arms and they walk back to his car. The thought of losing her daughter was far worse than anything she was about to face, therefore her feelings were not of fear, but of relief.

Hollywood, California

Tyler arrives back at his office after leaving his meeting with Gary. Sherri is sitting at her desk waiting for him to return with good news. Tyler walks in the office and she asks, "Well hey baby, how did it go?" "Did he fall for it?" Tyler's in such a rage he can barely look at her. He turns towards the wall with his fist to his forehead and eyes closed. "What's wrong honey is everything alright" asks Sherri? Tyler doesn't respond, giving her a deadly glance as he walks past her into his office.

Realizing something's wrong, Sherri decides not to press the issue. It's 4pm and Tyler is torn between conflicting emotions.

He wants to kill his Father-In-Law, he wants to kill his wife and now even feels like he should kill Sherri too because she knows too much. He now has to figure out how to get his wife back without her finding out his involvement in her captivity.

Tyler paces back and forth in his office. He calls for Sherri on the speaker phone, "Sherri, can I see you in my office." His office building is full of people; any loud noises will be heard by the people who work in nearby offices. He knows he must not do anything to make Sherri scream.

"Sure baby, I'll be right in." Sherri says as she walks in his office. Once in the office, Tyler slams his door behind her, and quickly grabs her by the throat, pinning her to the wall behind the door. The force lifts her off the floor.

Barely able to speak, Sherri says, "TYLER WHAT ARE YOU DOING?" "SHUT UP!" "I think you've said quite enough" as he squeezes his hands around her throat even tighter. "YOU have fu#ked my life up you stupid b#$#h. everything I worked so hard to get is all gone because of YOU! I could KILL YOU for this!" Tyler releases his grip on her neck. Sherri slowly falls to the floor gasping for breath.

Coughing as she tries to catch her breath, she asks, "what are you talking about?", as she gasps for air, "what did I do?" Holding her throat, totally puzzled, she looks at him for answers. Furious, he says, "I'LL TELL YOU WHAT YOU DID YOU STUPID Bi#@h, as he kicks her on the side of her stomach, while she's still on the floor.

"YOU Fu#%ed MY WHOLE fu#%ing PLAN UP YOU WORTHLESS PIECE OF Sh%t, you just couldn't", he kicks her in the face, "keep", kicking her again, "your f#%&in mouth closed!" kicking her a fourth time as blood flows from Sherri's nose and mouth.

She lays on the floor bleeding, barely able to move, while he paces back and forth across the room with his hands against his forehead, thinking how to get rid of her, if possible. In a rage he has an idea. He walks over to her and grabs a hand full of her hair and pulls her head from the floor so she can see his face. "Wake up!" She is dazed and almost unconscious. He shakes her, "I said wake up you stupid piece of sh#t; "because of you running you fu#@ing mouth, I now have to find a way to get my wife out of that warehouse without her finding out that I'm the one who put her there!"

"So now you listen to me, as he pulls her hair tighter and twists her neck. Since you're the one who shot her, you're going to be the one who rescues her. You were beaten by some crazy maniac and taken to the other side of the building and placed in an abandoned brick room just like the one she's in, and somehow you managed to get away to look for her, to save her before this crazy maniac returns. You have no idea who this maniac is; you just know he's very dangerous!" Tyler describes the scenario.

"Now let me make this clear b$#@h if my wife finds out that I had anything to do with this, I'll kill you!" "And then I'll bury your body so far away from here that no one will ever find your bones. Don't f%#k with me b$#@h because I am your crazy maniac!" He yells.

"When this office building shuts down tonight, you and I are going to take a little trip to that warehouse, and you're going to do exactly what I tell you to do, and if you f$#k this up", as he reaches in his pants pocket and pulls out a pocket knife, he puts it against her face, "I will f$#k you up!" He warns her.

"Understand this" he says as he leans over to whisper in her ear, "If you try to run, I will find you, I will be behind every door you ever crawl behind, I will be in your dreams as your worst nightmare. All you have to do is what I tell you to do, and you'll be just fine."

"The connection you claimed to get all your information about Gary from, worked for Gary and not only does Gary know about me, but he also knows about you too darling, so if I go down, you best believe I'm dragging you're a#s with me.

Now unless we get this woman back in perfect health, we're both going down, and I don't plan on going down, so you'll do whatever I tell you to do. Tyler drops her head and walks back to his desk to wash her blood from his hands. Sherri collapses, her face bloodied and bruised.

Tyler walks over to his door and looks back at her, "now you go ahead and get your rest darling, we've got a big night ahead of us." Leaving her unconscious on the floor, he walks out of his office locking the door behind him. He straightens his collar in front of his door and thinks to himself, "This sh#t better work!" as he leaves the building.

Seattle, Washington

Hell's fury is at a raging flame against Karen, and everything that can be shaken in her life, will be shaken. Karen's daughter, Rachael, is at the mall shopping when one of hells finest approaches her. Rachael is window shopping at the jewelry store and sees some beautiful necklaces. A stranger walks up to her and stands behind her looking over her shoulder. "They're gorgeous aren't they?" The stranger inclines.

Startled, she turns around to see whose talking. "Oh, yes, they are...very beautiful." "I'm sorry if I startled you; I couldn't help but notice the beauty in front of the beauty." The stranger says as he gives her a charming half smile. Blushing, Rachael stutters, uh- uh- um no -no really it's ok."

The stranger replies. "If you don't mind me asking, why would such a charming individual as yourself, stand graciously in front of a window of beauty; without her Prince Charming to accompany her?" Not impressed by his weak compliment. "Well, I guess I just love to window shop, and prince charming is at work, so he couldn't be here to accompany me today, but I'm sure he'll make up for it.

"If you'll excuse me, I really must be going!" As she tries to walk past the stranger, he tries again. "Ok, wait; wait I'm- I'm sorry- it's just that I'm an old romantic who unfortunately has very little experience with pickup lines." He smiles. "That's- not what I wanted to say either". "I've embarrassed myself now." Rachael smirks. "Please- please allow me to start over; as you can see this is not my area of expertise." The stranger says honestly.

He glances at her library card on the side of her purse and builds his identity from it. "Let me introduce myself, I am Professor Mirado. I have a private Library across town east of here, somehow I wandered away from work and ran into this beautiful jewel, whom I've managed to make a complete imbecile of myself in front of. Rachael becomes interested.

"Really, "WOW!" "That's great- Look I guess we did kind of start off on the wrong page. I'm Rachael and I must say it's a pleasure to meet you." She says intrigued. "On the contrary my dear, the pleasure indeed is all mine." He says smiling knowing that he has her attention.

"I just love exploring different authors and learning about their strengths and weaknesses; it's so inspiring to me to learn of all their endeavors to success." She explains. "Aah, if that's your passion, you will love my library of authors."

He says with a charming yet devious smile. "You have your own Library of authors?" Rachael says impressed. "Do I? One of the most prestigious Libraries on the east side; of course that's just my opinion, but I believe so." He says proudly. "That's amazing; I would love to see it." Rachael says.

"Funny you should ask", feeling more at ease about his quest for her, "if it's not too forward of me, would you join me for lunch at Shantii's, It just so happens that it was my next stop anyway; afterwards you could visit my Library and there you can read to your heart's content." "As they say; no strings attached." he smiles pleasantly.

Indecisive about his offer, "oh, I- I don't really, I don't think; the professor interrupts her. "My darling, I'm not asking you for your hand in marriage, I'm merely asking you to lunch; although that wouldn't be such an awful idea, I merely want to captivate your attention with a particular author who happens to be one of my favorites. I'm sure you'll feel the same as well." "I guess that should be alright, I mean I am quite intrigued with the authors." She replies,

"Excellent!" "Well now, how shall we do this, you could follow me there or we could take my car, I certainly couldn't ride with you; that wouldn't be too gentleman-like, now would it?" He smiles as he gazes deeply into her eyes. She releases a small chuckle, "I do understand, I can follow you there."

"Aww" He says playfully frowning. "I was so hoping you would choose to ride with me." "And why were you hoping that; what kind of car do you drive?" She responds playfully. Deviously smiling, "What car do you fancy the most?" Surprised by the question, "Me- um, I drive a little two door Honda, it's not much, but it works for me." Slightly frowning, "Perhaps you misunderstood me; I asked about the car you fancied most, not the car you drive."

"Oh, I'm sorry, I thought you meant my car, looking away thinking about it, I don't know, I guess-well I do love Porsches, it's my absolute dream car, and it's just as I said, dream car. A car I only dream of having." She laughs.

"I see we share the same taste." He says. "You drive a Porsche- really? "Wow!" A man after my own heart" she says excited. "Indeed!" He says confidently. "Well, highly impressed with his taste. I guess that changes everything, I guess I am riding with you then." She says with a flirty smile. "I guess you are." "Well then, shall we?" He holds out his arm and she puts her arm through his, and they head towards the exit talking and laughing.

At the parking deck, Rachael begins to look around for his Porsche. "So, where's you Porsche, what color is it?" getting excited. "What color do you fancy the most?" "Well, you might think I'm a little weird if I told you the colors I like." She explains. "Amuse me" He asked needing to hear her response.

"O- K you asked for it- I like, well, it's like a purplish color base with a smoky finish at the bottom and dark windows and a smoky purple like finish on the seat covers and floor mats." "See, I told you it was weird, I just have this thing for purple" she says with a half-smile un- sure of his thoughts.

"You are quite the amazing women, and rather scary if I might add, it seems you must have dreamed about my car, in order to describe it in such detail." "GET- OUT!" - For Real, "OH" my- you're joking right?" "You do not have that color car, "Oh My Gosh", Are you serious? You're kidding right", she says in unbelief of the strange coincidence.

"Well, as they say actions, speak louder than words." He smiles and taps his finger against his leg, while she looks around the parking deck for his car. As he tapped twice, the car appears on the third row of the parking deck.

"Ah, there it tis; is that the dream car you were speaking of?"

Totally in awe, "O-MY-GOD..." Deviously smiling he whispers to himself, "Not exactly"- but close." She didn't realize what he had said because she was too overwhelmed by the car. "I can't believe it, its- it's the exact color I was talking about".

"Oh my- no wonder you didn't think it was weird. This is "SO" "Amazing! WOW!" "May I"? She asks. "Absolutely" He tosses her his keys. She unlocks the doors, and opens the driver side door. Looking at all of her described colors, she sits in the drivers' seat, slowly gliding her hands around the steering wheel and across the smoky purple colored seat covers, while gazing at the matching floor mats.

"I- love- you!" she says as she closes her eyes exhaling slowly with her head against the headrest. He Smiles deviously, "Oh- you will!" "I do hate to disturb this relationship between you and my car, but we must be going; we don't want to miss our reservations at Shantii's now do we?"

Rachael snapping out of her car trance, "Oh, yes of course, I guess you want your seat back right?" She says jokingly. He charmingly smiles, "Well if we plan to make our reservations in time, I would think that to be a rather good idea." As he helps her out of the driver's seat. Rachael takes his hand and loses herself in his eyes. Pulling her to her feet, he stares deeply into her eyes, the beauty of his bluish gray eyes, mesmerizes her.

Feeling almost compelled to kiss him; she pulls away, gently releasing his hand. He leads her around to the passenger's side of the car gently takes her hand again and helps her into the car, then reaches across her to fasten her seat belt.

The smell of his cologne dazzles her body, giving her the feeling of a warm sensation. She becomes overcome with the desire of his touch, she began to find herself wanting him so badly, as she closes her eyes and his face passes hers; her body begins to tremble, the fantasy of his touch rendered her body moist. He closes her door without touching her and walks back around to the driver's side of his car. As he opens the door, he gently taps his finger twice on the hood of the car and immediately she snaps out of her trance, remembering nothing. "Well now, shall we go?" He asks. "Absolutely" She agrees.

He starts the car, with thousands of ideas about the evening circling his head; he knows that the time is not yet at hand, for him to touch her. They exit the mall parking deck and drive to Shantii's for lunch.

Driving to Shantii's, he inquires, "Is it too warm in here for you, I could turn down the heat?" "Oh no, it's just fine. I still can't believe I'm riding in my dream car, this is like so amazing!" "I see you're easily impressed, that's a good thing." He smiles. "Well, not usually, I'm always told I'm the most difficult one to please." He laughs, "Difficult, I should say the least." "Tell me, Ra-chael is it? "I love the way you pronounce my name, yes it's Rachael" she smiles.

"Good, I find it rather disturbing to mispronounce someone's name, after all, no one responds to a name that's not their own. He continues, "So tell me Rachael, what course of dining do you fancy the most? What makes your mouth water?"

"I'm open. Really it doesn't matter." "I'm sure there's some type of food you fancy more than others." He searches, needing her response. "Um- uh- Brazilian; I love Brazilian food" "Wonderful choice!" "Now don't tell me that Shantii's is a Brazilian Restaurant." "Oh no, not at all, Shantii's serves a variety of different foods, Brazilian food just happens to be their specialty, that's why it's such a wonderful choice."

"You are really something; it's as if you know what I'm thinking before I even think of it." "Not quite, but I'm working on it." he smiles. Looking out of the windows from inside of his Porsche, the scenery looks very beautiful, but in reality everything looks extremely different from what she thinks she sees.

 He turns   down a road full of abandoned buildings, on both sides of the street. They pull up in front of a large brick building that appeared to have been deserted for years. The front of the building looks like it had been badly damaged by a fire.

"Well now, are you ready for your Brazilian dish?" He asked. From inside of his car she sees a different image of the buildings; she sees newly built building with beautiful landscaping and palm trees. "Oh yes, I certainly am" she says excited.

He smiles then taps his finger twice on the steering wheel and everything on the outside becomes as she sees it from the inside of his car. Brand new buildings with beautiful landscaping and planted palm trees. The burned out building is now an elegant restaurant with a large elegant sign the reads - *SHANJIJ"S*.

He opens his door and gets out of the car. Closing his door, he looks around carefully to see if all is well before he lets her out of his car. Down the road, he sees two homeless men walking, dressed like bums. He taps his finger twice on the hood of his car and instantly the men became business men dressed in business suits. Then he walks around to open her door for her. He extends his hand out to assist her from the car; she's takes his hand looking around overly amazed with the beauty of the area.

"it's all so beautiful, where are we, I've never seen anything like this in Seattle- Come on, palm trees in Seattle, they must be fake, how could they survive the weather we have here?" He takes her by the hand and escorts her into the building, "you mustn't believe everything that you see, I'm sure they are fake, after all, the weather is quite nasty here on earth- I mean, in Seattle." He says quickly correcting himself. "Real or fake, they are still the most beautiful things I've ever seen in Seattle" she says gazing around. "Thank you!" He replies.

"Why are you thanking me, it's not like you built this town?" She says jokingly. He laughs, "And, it isn't like I didn't." As they enter the restaurant they're greeted by the hostess who shows them to their table. "Oh my God this is so beautiful!" She says looking around.

"You use that expression quite often don't you? Why do you say that?" He asks a bit irritated. "Say what?" repeating her words, "Oh- My- God!" "I didn't realize I said it that much, I guess it's my way of expressing my feelings when something blows my mind, does it bother you when I say that?" "Oh no" He quickly responds, "just curious".

"Waiter," He signals for the waiter, "We're ready to order now; what would you fancy love?" She looks her menu, "do you serve rack of lamb?" The waiter was about to say no until Professor Mirado taps his finger twice under the table, "No, I- I mean yes we do" stumbles the waiter.

She looks at the menu frowning, "funny, I don't see it on the menu." He taps again under the table, "look again love", you'll find it on the second page of your menu." She looks again, "Oh, it's right here, how did I miss that. I must be losing it."

"No, you're just so excited." He smiles. Curiously she asks, "So you're not having anything?" "Oh yes of course, it's just that, this is one of my many spots to entertain, and they know my taste well." "So tell me about Rachael, what about you makes you so- you?" "I've never been asked that before. Let's see, well, I'm a psychology student, I go to school on campus and on line, which frees up a lot of my time and I'm single with no children."

"As I can recall, from our conversation at the mall this morning, your Prince Charming is at work preparing to make up his absence to you at a later time." He says smiling jokingly. Slightly embarrassed, "Oh that, forgive me, that's just something I say when I don't want to be bothered.

It normally works; you were just so persistent." Still smiling, "I knew you weren't being honest with me. That was the purpose of my persistence." "Tell me more, what about your family, what are they like? They must be very proud of you."

She smiles, "I'll say, my brother Samuel still treats me like a little girl." "Samuel- hum" he says with a half-smile. "Do you know him", she asks. "No, no not at all, it's just that I met a Samuel once, not long ago whom I offered a position, and somehow he managed to get away from me. Nevertheless, there's more where he came from!" He says looking at her intensely. "What kind of position did you offer him?"

"Nothing really to shout about, it was an old warehouse with a basement that processed a furnace that we often used, I offered him a position in the boiler room.", he laughs, "I could imagine it was a bit too hot for him, somehow or someone helped him get away; so I guess I'll just have to replace him. No biggie as they say. But as for now, I'm more interested in you; you're quite a lovely one. What about your parents, what are they like?"

Rachael says sadly, "Well my father was killed in an accidental fire at our family church." "Accidental you say", "and who may I ask, determined that?" He frowns. "Oh, I don't know, I think the coroners did I guess. I mean, how else could there have been a fire if it wasn't accidental?" She asks innocently, He becomes very serious, "perhaps someone close to you started it, have you ever considered that?"

 "Well, no- no not at all, why would someone we know want to start a fire at our church, I mean everybody loved my father!" Breathing rapidly, "Did your mother- love him?"

"My mother loved my father very much, he was her world, and she would've done anything for him. They were like a match made in heaven. His death really took her by surprise, she says that she can still see him and hear his voice at times. I think she believes that because she misses him so" She explains.

Hiding his rage, his body becomes hot as fire, she could see that his expressions had changed, and becomes concerned. Beneath the table he was about to tap his finger to destroy her when the waiter arrives with their dinner. "Are you ok, you seem a little upset, is it something I said?"

He closes his eyes and regains his composure. "No- no I'm fine, I just get a little heated when Justice is due, but yet protected by people in high places who yet follow orders from absent bosses; when in fact they should mind their own. He raises his finger, "Ah, the food has arrived, Bon apatite! He puts his finger back down. "Everything looks really great." She says smiling. "I'm delighted you're enjoying yourself."

"You know, the entire time I've been talking to you, I never bothered to ask you your first name, what is your name?" Looking intensely into her eyes, "My friends all call me Luther; believe it or not I'm actually a junior!" "So what does your father do?"

Smiling deviously, he states, "My father is the father of all fathers, he has many jobs. However, the one he's most active in is collections. He collects only what belongs to him, but he chases all of what doesn't. He's very good at what he does!" "And if you don't believe that, take a look at what he's done here."

He then taps his finger twice on the table in front of her, and instantly she becomes surrounded by blazing flames of hot fire all around her.

The fancy tiles in the floor began to break apart falling into the pit hole of Hell beneath it; square by square it rapidly fell in. She looks at her plate of food and saw a distorted face with worms coming from the mouth of it and maggots coming from the eyes. What she thought was a rack of lamb was actually a dead rat -worms and bugs.

She gags, coughing trying to vomit up the food she ate. Crying and screaming for help, bloody scared hands rising up from the pit of Hell, reached for her legs trying to pull her in. She looks at Professor Mirado as he transforms into something she would have never imagined; His body became as red as fire. His eyes turned white with burning flames in them. His skin was as that of dragon's scale.

From his head grew long fiery ram horns. His finger nails were as sharp as razors and fire red. His laugh was tormenting to the ears and everyone around her looked like demons with tails. Being pulled to the hole, she falls to the floor crying and screaming for God to help her. The Devil marks her plead for help, telling her that her God has forsook her and that she now belongs to them.

The arms from hell becomes too strong for her to fight off, and she begins to sink into the pit of Hell; screaming and kicking, with everything in her she finds just enough straight to pull her body from the pit by grabbing broken pieces of tile that had not yet broken off into the pit.

She managed to kick one of her legs a loose and proceeds to climb out. Just as she reaches the top with just one leg left to free, she hears someone calling her name from the pit. Refusing to look back she commences to climb out of pit of Hell. Kicking her other leg free, she reaches the top. With both of her knees on the floor of broken tile, she tries to crawl to safety but was interrupted by the voice she heard calling her name.

It was now right beside her face; she could feel the evil seeping from its pours. It whispers to her in a raspy voice saying; "My little girl has come home!" Frightened out of her mind she looks it in the face only to discover that it was her father Charles. She screams to the top of her lungs as he grabs her from behind her neck pulling her body backwards into the pit of Hell! Falling into the pit you could hear her screaming for miles down.

Suddenly, The Devil taps his finger twice against his leg and everything goes back to the way she first saw it. Lamb chops, sautéed asparagus and seasoned rice. A gorgeous restaurant and palm trees and she remembered nothing that was real.

"So tell me my dear, how was everything", he asks with a delightful smile? With a bright smile on her face, "Oh it was all so wonderful, we have to come back someday soon. I've had the most amazing time with you." she says gazing into his eyes.

Smiling intensely, "I certainly agree!" Waiter, check please" As the waiter walks over to their table he refuses to give him a check, "I'm sorry Mr. Mirado, your money is no good here, compliments of the chef." Professor Mirado looks at the waiter and smiles, "Thank you young man, you are all too kind." Looking over at her smiling, "Well then, shall we go?" He extends his hand out to her and helps her from her seat. Pulling her to her feet, she becomes lost in his eyes.

He gently pulls her close to him and passionately kisses her, feeling her body tremble at his touch, he slides his sharp red finger nails down her back as she presses her body closer to his. Gently pulling from the kiss his hands returned to a human state and he proudly walks her to the car knowing his mission is near completion.

Helping her in the car, they drive away, heading to his private library that she so eagerly wants to see. While everything behind them returns back to its desolate state at the tap of his finger as they drive away.

Brooklyn, New York

Zach and Bobby are across town near where Candy's boyfriend was shot, asking questions. "Yo dog, I got a partner of mine who stay close by here, it's Larry, you know em, dat nigga is like the CNN News he know 'bout everything." Zach tells him. "Sh#t, let's hit dat nigga up den, so we can get to the bottom of dis sh#t."

"Let me call dat fool and see where he at." Zach says as he dials the number on his cell phone. Larry answers, "Yeah", Zach replies, "What's up nigga?" "Nothing much dog, what's going on with you", Larry asks? "I'm out your way, you busy? I gotta a nigga on da radar; we wanna know what you know" Zach says. "Who is it", Larry asks? "Dat's what I'm trying to find out from you", Zach replies. "Who's with you", Larry asks? "Just me and my boy Bobby." "Tell Bobby what's up. Y'all can swing through and we can check it out."

They get in the car and head to Zac's boy's house. They arrive ten minutes later and walk up to his apartment door in the projects. Zach knocks on the door. Larry opens the door; they shake hands, "what's up dog, long times no hear from. What you been up to Bobby", Larry says. "Chillin...chillin, Where yo girl at Larry, Bobby asks? "Man I drop dat b#@$h about a month ago. One of my partners caught her wit one of his niggas, I tried to kill dat hoe!" Bobby replies, "d$#n man, dat sh#t is f#$@%d up."

"I know right! Dat bi#@h f#$%ed up, she gonna miss this dick and paper, cause dat nigga she fu#%#n wit ain't about sh#t he treat her like s#@t, but dat's on her dog, I can't f$#k with her no mo", Larry explains. "I heard that", Bobby says. "So what you got going on Zach?" Larry asks

Zach runs down the situation, "my boy Tyrone, I don't think you know him; anyway, he been f#%&in wit some crazy chick who lost her baby daddy in a shootout, and he wanna find the nigga who did it, so that he can take em out."

Larry frowning in confusion, "what kind of sh#t is dat, why the f*&k is he trying to take

168

out her baby daddy's murderer, who the f$#k is dis b#$%h- you said it's her baby's daddy; so the baby ain't his and he wanna take out the nigga dat killed her baby daddy, was he f#%&in her baby's daddy too? Cause ain't no way I'm gonna take out a nigga because of some crazy b#$@h's nigga. Dat s#$t ain't making no sense, cuz!."

Zach shakes his head, "you preaching to the fu#@in choir dog, I just said f$#k it, I ain't even trying to figure dat sh@t out no mo dog. Tyrone's my boy, so if taking dis nigga out is gonna do it for him, then f$#k it let's just do dis sh#t." Larry gives them some free advice, "you need to check your boy, sounds to me like he might be a little sweet." Zach replies, "dat's on him dog, I ain't got s$#t to do with who he f#%&in."

Larry asks, "So how are we supposed to find his boyfriends killer?" Zach and Bobby laugh. "Well... this s#$t sound crazy to me", Larry says laughing.

Zach agrees, "dis s*&t do sound crazy yo." Larry trying to figure it out, "crazy ain't the "f#%&in word, GAY is more like da word for that nigga. Does yo boy know who did it?"

"Naw man, he said dat, ole boy called out his killer's name to somebody before he died; we trying to find out who was with him when he died." Zach explains. "When did all dis sh#t take place" Larry asks. "He said about five or six months ago. He said, ole boy was driving down da Street shooting in the air and sh#t and somebody capped his a#s."

Larry tries to remember, "seems like I heard about sum sh#t like dat; yeah, yeah dat was one of Luke's boy's dat got hit dat night; a cat name Tony, if we talking about da same cat- yeah that's him.

Something about he and his girl having a baby, or wanting a baby or some sh#t like dat, she told him he was gonna be a daddy, and dat nigga drove down da street shooting in the air. I forgot what Tony's girl's name was, but I heard dat b#$@h was fine!" Zach inquires, "was her name Candy?" "Yeah, dat was her name, Candy, you know her?"   "Naw, I didn't know her, she dat crazy b#$@h I told you my boy Tyrone's f#@&ing with."

With his fist at his mouth laughing, "Aw sh#t dog, yo boy might not be gay after all, if she look like da say she look, hell I guess I'd shoot dat nigga too." Laughing along, Bobby says, "boy you crazy- I never met her, but I met her crazy mamma though."

"So dat's why my boy got his nose all up in da air, dat nigga's p@$$ywhipped!" They all break out laughing. "Larry starting to realize,

Y'all looking for da same nigga Luke been looking for, he said he know where dat nigga live. I ain't heard no more about it though, but knowing Luke, he might have him set up already, cause dat's another crazy motherf#@*er, he ain't got sh#t else to do but kill nigga's" Larry explains.

Bobby adds, "well sh%t if Luke got em already, we ain't got to worry about dis s$#t no mo , let dat crazy motherf#@$*r handle it." "Where is Luke now?" Zach asks.

"Your guess is as good as mine, dat nigga might be on somebody's f#%&in beach drinking a bottle of Dom somewhere. He ain't never in one place; dat nigga got so much paper, he got fools everywhere taking mother#@#s out!" Larry replies. "Well sh#t let dat nigga handle dat motherfu#%er then, dat's less blood for me to spill." Zach says.

 "We gotta get back to our side of town and handle sum other sh#t we got going on. But I'll hit you back and let you know what's up." "Ok cool dat's what's up and if I hear anything else about ole boy, I'll hit you up." Larry says. They all shake hands, "all right Larry we out." They leave the apartment. Zach and Bobby get back in the car headed back to their side of town.

New Hope, Virginia

Grandma Ames's trip to Washington

Sunday Morning, Grandma Ames and her daughter Brenda are in church, when the Pastor calls her out. Only the faithful ten members are in the sanctuary. "It's good to see my faithful few here today. God will truly honor your obedience in coming to the house of the Lord. It is our heart's desire that brings us here today and it is our true heart's desire that will keep us coming".

"Amen", Brenda says. "Sister Ames, will you come to the front of the church please?" Grandma Ames walks to the front of the church and stands in front of the Pastor. "Yes Pastor?"

He looks her in the eyes and holds her hands, "The Lord showed me a vision of you traveling west, and he showed me three others who were with you; he said to follow you on your journey for it is he who put you on this path and it is he who will deliver you from the enemy's hands." Grandma Ames starts praising God for the confirmation. "Thank you Lord Jesus, Thank you, Thank you, Halleluiah, Halleluiah Thank you Jesus, Thank ya", she shouts.

"Come on saints of God, give Him some Glory, Thank him for his goodness, thank him for his Mercy, come on and help me bless his Holy name. Glory to God, Halleluiah, come on and give him the Glory, for he's worthy of all the praise."

"Come on, Come on, Come on, you can do better than that, come on and magnify the Lord with me, let us exalt his name together, Halleluiah, Halleluiah, Halleluiah", the Saints of God worship him from their hearts.

After the church service was over, the Pastor calls a meeting with the members in his office to discuss the vision from the Lord. "Saints I called you here today because we are in a warfare and only the strong will survive, Sister Ames, were you aware that God wants you to travel west", Pastor asks?

"Yes sir Pastor, the Lord appeared to me in the Spirit and told me; 'As far as the east is from the west he wanted me to travel there to stand in the path of the righteous'. He said that it is a good fight of faith. Everything you said to me today Pastor, the Lord told me in the spirit". She says.

"Praise the Lord! God is truly a faithful God. Well, Sister Ames, he told me to follow you and there will be two more who will follow us. Among this group, who will follow us", asks Pastor? "Momma, why didn't you tell me you were going to Washington, are you sure you want to go there, it's quite a ways from here momma?" Brenda says.

"When the Lord tells you to go baby, you got to go, no question about it!" Grandma Ames says. Brenda continues "Ok, so when are we leaving", "Brenda baby, this is not a trip that you are prepared to take; you will have to sit this one out." "Momma, I'm not about to let you travel all the way across the world by yourself; anything could happen to you out there!"

"First of all, I am not alone nor will I be alone, did you not hear Pastor when he said there are three others who will follow me. You can't tamper with the will of God baby." "Why do you feel that I'm not prepared to take this trip?"

"Brenda baby, by you asking me if I'm sure about going to Washington, you have shown me that you're not strong enough to go, because when God says go, who are we to question that? I don't know why or who I am going there for, but it has to be serious if God made a special trip down to visit with the Pastor and me."

You best be quiet and obedient and just stay put, because what God puts in place, you don't want to be the one who's in the way of it baby."

Brenda humbles herself, "Yes ma'am I do understand, I'll stay home." "Your mother's right Brenda, this has to be a big deal if he had to make a personal visit. The Lord said "Only the Strong will survive, and if you have any doubt in your hearts or mind, about your spiritual walk with God; Please do not attempt to travel on this path of the righteous! Is there anyone else who's sure about their spiritual walk and is ready for this great Battle", Pastors asks?

Co-Pastor Carl McPheir testifies, "I will follow you." Sister Yolanda, prayer intercessor agrees, "I will follow you too." "Then that settles it, we will meet back here in the morning to discuss the details of this trip. I'm asking everyone to fast and pray for one week before we take our journey." Pastor instructs.

"I don't know what we're going to come face to face with, but whatever it is, we must be ready and willing to fight that good fight of faith." "God has equipped us to defeat the enemy, therefore we must do our parts and be ready, cause I just got a feeling that we are about to experience something bigger than we've ever dealt with in our lives", Grandma Ames expresses.

Pastor explains, "I need for everyone who's staying behind to be in prayer for us at all times during this battle, we all must come together as one voice in the spirit; in order to break the strong holds." All the saints agree and are preparing for the big battle.

Atlanta, Georgia

Tammy turns herself in

Robert and Tammy back out from the dirt road onto the streets heading towards town. "I'm going to call my lawyer today so I can make sure he gets you out of the jail as soon as possible, because that's not where you need to be." Not caring, "Robert, really, it's ok, it doesn't matter where they put me or what they do to me, it still won't compare to what's already done."

"It does matter what they do to you, you were strictly acting out of hurt and grief, no judge will put you in jail for that, you're not a criminal you're a decent mother who lost her only child. You don't think that's not enough to drive someone insane?" Starting to cry again, "she wasn't just my only child, she was my reason to really live, to get up in the mornings, to go to work, my everything. What's the purpose now, it's all just routine."

"You're just talking out your head right now, you don't mean any of this. And even if you did, I'm not just going to sit back and watch you waste away to nothing, what kind of brother or even human being would I be to let that happen?", "I'm going to take care of you and like I said, I am not going to let anything happen to you. Just lean on me little sis, I got you."

Tammy lays her head on the passenger side window staring into space with her eyes full of tears. They arrive at the Atlanta Police Precinct, Robert gets out of the car, "wait here Tammy, I'll be right back." Tammy sits there in a daze. Entering the Precinct he walks over to the front desk officer. "Can I speak to the lieutenant?" "What's your name sir?", "Robert Johnson sir." "What's this concerning Mr. Johnson?" "It's a private Matter that really needs the lieutenants' attention."

"The Lieutenant is busy; you'll have to come back." Robert says sternly, sir, if you value your position at this Precinct, I suggest you think twice before letting me walk away, the consequences could be great!" "Sir, are you threatening me?" The officer says defensively. "Look!" "I don't have time for this, either you let me speak to the Lieutenant right now or I will walk out of here and not come back. The next time you hear my name or yours will be on channel 5, news for letting a wanted person escape for the second time', Robert says loudly.

The commotion in the precinct causes everyone to focus on Robert and the officer. Lieutenant Larson walks through the door, not knowing the situation, sees his officer arguing with another person, and walks over to intervene. "What seems to be the problem here?"

Turning towards the lieutenant, Robert explains, I politely asked this officer to speak to the Lieutenant, concerning a private matter; he gets rude with me and tells me to come back another time because the lieutenant is busy.

He didn't ask to take my information nor did he offer me to speak with the next officer in charge, I don't appreciate his attitude towards me just because he wears a badge."

Politely, Lieutenant Larson, says, "Well sir, I do apologize for my officer, however I'm Lieutenant Larson, what can I do for you." Robert calms down, "Can I speak to you in private sir?" Looking concerned, "Sure, come with me." He leads Robert to an office just down the hall on the right. "Have a seat, now what is it you need to speak to me about?"

"Lieutenant, are you familiar with the Hospital episode that took place a few days ago?" "Are you referring to the attempted murder case at Southern General Hospital?" "Yes that's the one." "Very much so,-" What about it?" "Well, that woman on the run is my sister. I just wanted to give you a little insight into the situation. My sister is a decent citizen; she's been working at that hospital for over 15 years, and was very loved by everyone.

She only had one child, a daughter, my niece. As Roberts' eyes begin to water he continues, "Like most teenage girls, Rhonda got involved with the wrong boy at school, one that the police were searching for. My sister tried to keep Rhonda away from that boy, but Rhonda loved him. The reason the police was after that boy, was because he had A.I.D.S, and he was freely spreading it around to different girls."

Lieutenant Larson frowns, "I think I remember that case. For some reason that boy had a way of getting past us every time we got close to him, I think he had a lot of people helping him."

Robert says, "Well, that boy was carrying everything, not just A.I.D.S. and everything that he had, he gave to my niece, Tammy's daughter. When my sister found out about it, she took her daughter to the doctor's office to see how bad it was. The doctor ran tests on her, and told them that the additional diseases contracted from him, made the A.I.D.S virus deadlier, leaving my niece with less than one year to live."

After my sister heard the news she passed out, then my niece was so distraught about the news, she grabbed a scalpel from one of the draws in the doctor's office and sliced her own throat while her mother was still passed out. When her mother regained conscious, seeing her daughter on the floor traumatized her to the point that she lost her mind."

A week later at the funeral reception a strange woman walked in my sister's home asking me to speak to her, we didn't know who she was, and I thought this lady would be a good comfort for my sister, because she told me that a similar thing happened to her child. I had no idea that she was that boy's mother!

There was a big commotion on the patio, when I got to her, Tammy was going crazy on that woman, screaming 'you killed my daughter', Tammy beat her up so bad the woman ended up in the hospital. They didn't know that they took the woman to same hospital where Tammy works.

When Tammy found out about it, she tried to take the life of the woman, who in her mind took her daughter's life. That's why my sister did what she did, she's not a criminal. She's a mother who loved her daughter. She only ran because of fear and even then she didn't know where to go, because she was only used to going to work and home.

I just want to make sure she doesn't sit in jail, when she really needs mental help to help her let go of her daughter's death".

After hearing Robert describes the details of what happened, Lieutenant Larson's heart was touched, "I'm so sorry to hear this. I can only imagine what your sister must be going through, where is she now?" Feeling more at ease, Robert, says, "I told her that this isn't what her daughter would have wanted for her mother, and I convinced her to turn herself in. She's outside in my car now." "Right now!" he says a little concerned.

Robert assures him, "you really don't have to worry about her running again, because in the state of mind she's in I don't think she knows or even cares where she's at or what happens to her, because she says the worst has already been done." Feeling sympathy for Tammy, the lieutenant wants to help her, "Well let's go get her out of your car, we don't want her doing anything crazy to herself."

Robert and the Lieutenant Larson leave the office together; he follows Robert to his car. When they arrive at the car, Tammy is still laying carelessly against the car door window. Robert slowly opens the door and holds her head, so that she didn't fall out of the car. He grabs her arm helping her out of the car.

She's like dead weight and begins to fall to the ground, Lieutenant Larson rushes over to assist him, grabbing Tammy by the other arm. They help her into the precinct, and assist her to the bench. "Get me an ambulance now", the lieutenant says as he frowns at the front desk officer. "Yes sir!" The front desk officer calls the ambulance.

Lieutenant Larson tries to talk to Tammy, "Ms. Johnson my name is Lieutenant Larson, I'm going to get you some help, do you understand me." Tammy sits with her head back against the wall, with tears in her eyes. "I think she's getting worse by the minute", Lieutenant Larson says.

Robert sits beside her, pulls her in his arms, her head falls to his shoulder. "Tammy it's me, Robert your brother, don't do this to me Tammy, come on now, we're going to get past this, but I need you to be strong for me. Tammy I don't want to lose you girl, I need you to talk to me. Robert gently grabs her by the face and looks in her eyes, "Tammy come on baby, you have to snap out it sweetheart, I love you Tammy, don't leave me now baby, I need you to stay with me baby", rubbing her arm, "come on baby girl, stay with your big brother, stay with me", Robert pleads.

The ambulance arrives at the Precinct; they bring in a stretcher and strap Tammy in. As they carry her to the back of the ambulance, before they put her in, Robert grabs her by her hand and talks to her, "Tammy, baby, they're going to take very good care of you baby. Please don't give up sweetheart; I can't handle losing you Tammy.

I need you to pull through this baby girl. I can't lose you too baby, As Robert lies his head on her chest, he begs, "I just can't do it." Lieutenant Larson helps Robert up from beside the stretcher. They put the stretcher in the back of the ambulance and head toward the hospital. Lieutenant Larson walks Robert into his office reassuring him that she would get the best care. Robert sits in the chair with his elbows to his knees and his face in his hands crying. Lieutenant Larson's eyes became watery at the sight of Robert's broken heart.

Hollywood, California

The Rescue

While Tyler's away from his office, Sherri regains consciousness. Realizing where she is, she tries to get up from the floor, but still feels sharp pains on her side and ribs. It becomes harder to breath. Between breaths, she painfully slides her body to Tyler's desk, trying to reach the phone.

The Warehouse

Across town, Susan is losing her strength and has become very weak. A homeless man who's looking for a place to make a home for the night, wanders into the warehouse where Susan is captured. Entering the building, he hears someone screaming. He makes his way to the back of the building where he heard the screaming. He comes to a locked door of an abandoned brick room. The homeless man says cautiously, "who's in here?" Susan hears his voice, "In here, I'm in here, please help me, I can't move my leg and I'm very weak." "How did you get in here", the homeless man asks?

"I don't know, I woke up a couple of days ago in here, I don't know who put me in here or what happened to me. Please, I need your help, please help me." The homeless man tries to open the lock but cannot get it open. He looks around and finds a medium size piece of concrete. Carrying the concrete piece over to the door: "hold on a minute, I gotta try to get this lock undone." "OK, please hurry!"

He bangs the concrete against the lock several times, breaking the lock. The moment freezes and things became still. Mercy and Grace appear in front of the brick door while the moment is frozen. Grace says in a deep voice, "Mercy, why are you disobeying orders, for your presence here is before it's time."

Mercy says in a deep voice, "my brother Grace, have you not eyes to see, nor a heart to feel that which is at hand. Is it possible to turn your eyes from that which is right?"

Grace continues, "Your presence here at this time is not welcome, return thy self now to the Holy ones appointed to our watch, that your disobedience may be forgiven." Grace and Mercy leaves the area and the homeless man disappears. Susan takes her last breath and dies.

Back at the office, Sherri struggles to reach the phone. The extreme pain causes her to pass out again before she could dial a number. One hour later, Tyler returns and finds Sherri unconscious behind his desk, with the phone receiver hanging from his desk beside her. Tyler snatches the phone and listens to see if anyone is on the other end. He slams the phone down on the base. You stupid b#$%h who the hell did you call? He picks her up and places her lifeless body on the couch in his office.

Looking in her face, he sees no signs of life, so he checks her neck for a pulse. Finding a pulse he becomes relieved and tried to wake her up. "Sherri, wake up", smacking her face, "wake up Sherri." He carefully rocks her head from side to side, "wake up Sherri, wake up." Feeling a little scared he walks over to his desk and grabs his bottle of water, he goes back to the couch, pours the water onto her face. Sherri starts to cough, as she tries to open her eyes. Tyler's so glad she isn't dead that he kisses her on the forehead.

"Oh thank goodness, you're alive, I'm so sorry I did this to you, you didn't deserve this, come on open your eyes", Tyler begs. Sherri opens her eyes and looks at Tyler. He pulls her by the arm trying to sit her up, "come on Sherri sit up."

Sherri screams in pain," OOOH, HH, OWCH." Tyler lays her back on the couch, "where does it hurt?" Sherri is barely able to speak, "it's my ribs, I think they're broken aahh, I need a doctor." Tyler realizes that his plan has taken a turn for the worse. Pacing back and forth, he tries to think of different alternatives.

Tyler rushes back over to Sherri, "do you think you can walk?" In much pain, "I don't uh think so." Tyler tries to lift her again, "come on you have to try, how can I get you to a doctor if you can't walk." Sherri pushes through her pain, thinking he's trying to get her to a doctor, ok, hhh, uh I'm trying."

In a panic, Tyler pulls her to her feet, she screams in pain. "See now, I knew you could do it. All you have to do is stand here and breath slow. We're going to walk to the elevator and go down to my car. Then I can take you to the hospital, but you have to stay conscious and do what I say, or else we'll never make it there."

With her body racking in pain, she believes him. She gives it everything she has, "ok, I'm going to try, it hurts so bad Tyler" "I know, but we have to keep moving if you want to get some help", he says. Tyler remembers the cameras in the office building hallway near the elevator.

Thinking fast, he grabs an over coat from his office closet, and throws it over her shoulders, and grabs a bottle of wine from his cabinet. Walking out the office with her, he closes the door behind him. Slowing walking through the halls, he holds the bottle of wine in the hand that's holding Sherri up, acting as if she's drunk. While waiting for the elevator, he begins kissing her as if they were together having fun.

Tyler whispers in her ear while kissing her, "stay with me, we're half way there." The elevator door opens, and they slowly step inside. When the doors close he turns to Sherri and looks into her eyes."

Come on Sherri, stay with me, we only have a little further to go before we get to my car." In great pain she whispers, "Ok I am."

Arriving at his car, Tyler unlocks the doors and gently lays Sherri in the back seat. Throwing the bottle of wine on the floor board of the back seat, he starts the car and heads out of the parking deck. Sherri passes out again. He looks back at her and sees her passed out, and drives across town to the warehouse.

Brooklyn, New York

The Price to pay

Tyrone is in his living room when he gets a call, "Hello, who is this; yeah this is him, say what now? Asking for me? How soon, aight, no problem I'll be there as soon as I can, yeah! He hangs up.

He walks to his bedroom and prepares to take a shower. He picks out a nice shirt and some slacks; he lays the clothes across his bed, as he goes in to take a shower. While in the shower he hears a noise, he stops washing his face to listen. Hearing nothing he continues to wash his face and head.

About three minutes later he hears the sound of the door closing. Becoming curious, he steps out of the shower and grabs his towel, wrapping it around his waist. He slowly walks over to his nightstand and grabs his gun from the drawer. Easing the drawer shut he removes the safety lock from his gun. With his back against the wall, he slowly moves towards his kitchen.

Hearing something moving in the kitchen, he leaps from behind the wall with his gun drawn. freeze Mother#@%er"! "turn around b#%#h"!

His friend Mike turns around with his hands up, dropping the box of milk he was drinking, replies. "I got your b%#ch", "b%#ch!"

189

lowering the gun, "What da f#%k you doing man? I almost shot yo a#s boy."

Mike puts his hands down, "who else has a gotd%mn key to yo gotd%mn apartment fool." Holding his towel, "you can't be sneaking up on a nigga like dat boy, dat's the way to get yo a#s shot! "I didn't know who the f%$k you waz!" "I thought somebody was trying to rob me or some s#%t". Mike picks up the milk carton he dropped when Tyrone yelled freeze. "Rob what, nigga, you ain't got s#$t in here to take." A mother#@$er try to rob you, he gonna shoot you for wasting his time breaking in."

Holding the towel around his waist, "whatever fool, I must got something, yo a#s keep hanging around." "That's because I ain't got s#$t else to do", "And why the f#%k you walking around in a towel anyway, what, the f#%k did you think, if da gun don't work you gona terrorize them by dropping the towel", Mike laughs.

Tyrone walks back to his room, "naw fool, I wuz taking a shower before the milk man tried to f$#@in rob me." Mike walks over to the couch to watch TV yells back at him. "Cause dat's about the only thing worth robbing in dis motherf#@%er." "where da hell you going anyway?" Tyrone yells from the shower, "I got a call dis morning from da Hospital, Candy wants to see me." Shocked, "Candy" She out?"

"No but apparently she's doing better if she can have visitors", Tyrone replies. "Why all of a sudden she wanna see you?" "What you mean all of a sudden, I told you she still love me".

"All dat s$#t you wuz talking about her not given a f$#k about me, now you see." Mike shakes his head, "I still say dat girl is trouble dog."

Tyrone walks out of the bedroom all dressed, fastening his watch around his wrist, "and I still say you paranoid." Mike drinks a beer, "you want me to roll wit you just in case she think you dat nigga, and tries to attack you." Ignoring his comment, "you can ride, but not for dat reason."

They leave the house headed to the hospital. An hour later they arrive at the hospital. They both get out of the car and walks into the hospital. As they enter the building Mike sees Candy's mother in the sitting area. "Isn't that that crazy bi#%h me saw at Candy's house?" Looking around, yeah that's her crazy a%s mother!" They stop by the waiting room to speak to her before they went to the front desk.

Tyrone greets Candy's mom, "what's up miss lady?" Candy's mom turns to look at him, "you finally made it, I thought you would never get here." Frowning he replies, "what you talking about get here? How da f$#k you know I was coming?" "Cause I'm da one who called you're a##". Mikes looks at him in discuss, "See!" I told you dat sh#t didn't sound right. Dat b#$@h got to much f u%&in game."

"I ain't got no muthaf$#@ing game fool, I'm trying to visit my daughter; but da don't believe that I'm her mother and I lost my fu%#in ID, so I had to find somebody who can identify me as her mother. The only one I could think about waz you!"

Mike looking discussed, "Why da f$#k are you trying to see her now; all dat talk about you not giving a f$#k about what happens to dat bi#@h and now all of a sudden you her f*#@in mother. B#@$h you ain't nothing but a game playing trick!"

Ignoring him, "I ain't going there with you today Mike!" I wasn't trying to play no fu#%in games with you, but I knew you wouldn't come here if you knew it was me."

Tyrone is angry, "you d#%n right I wouldn't come here for you!" "You one skanky muthaf^%$a!" "Why you wanna play on yo own daughter like dat?" "I'm telling you da truth, I really want to see Candy ."

Mike still discussed, "what da f#@k for?" "What she got dat you want now, and why da f#@k would we help you anyway?" becoming irritated with him, "I didn't ask YOU to do sh#t for me Mike!" "Ok den, why da f$#k would HE help you "anyway?" Turning to look at Tyrone, listen to me, they're transferring Candy to another Hospital today, and I just wanted to see her before they moved her!"

Looking concerned, "Where the f$#k are da taking her?" She Whispers, "I don't know, but I was thinking, if we followed the van she's in, we could hit it up and get her out, and y'all could get the f%$k out of dodge before they even know she's gone." Seriously considering it, "how would we know what van she's in?"

Mike becomes instantly pissed off, "You gotta be f#%&in kidding me dog, are you f$#kin serious!" You really fu#%in thinking about doing dat sh#t?" "Have you lost yo Mutherfu#%in mind T"?

"What part of bulls#@t does dis not sound like?" "Dis bi%#h don't give a fu#k about dat girl, and you know dat cuz, so why da f*&k are you even thinking bout dis sh#t?"

Mike geting ready to walk out, "You know what, y'all go right ahead and knock you self the f@#k out with dis s*&t, but if dat's how you finna roll, you just lost me dog, cause dis is bullsh#t!" "Hold up Mike, I never said I was down wit dis s#@t cuz, I just asked a f@#$in question, why you tripping?"

"T, how long have we been boyz?" And how much Sh%t have we been f#%&in through together? And you don't think I know yo as%, you never ask questions unless you thinking bout making s#@t happen.

"So you go right ahead and think the f*&k on, G, I'm f#%&in out!" Mike walks out of the hospital. As he walks out, three boys with hoodies on, walk in. Tyrone is talking to Candy's mom with his back towards the door. As they're talking, Candy is being escorted to the van. Passing through the hall's she sees the three boys with hoodies on and she speaks to one of them. While the orderlies are signing Candy's transfer papers, she sees Tyrone in the waiting area and calls out to him.

"Hey baby." He looks around and sees her standing there and goes over to meet her. "Candy!" oh baby, I missed you so much." He picks her up and spins her around and kisses her. "Guess what baby, they're letting me go home with you, I'm free baby, I'm free." He

194

smiles in amazement. "Oh wow, dat's great ma, I can't wait to get you home." He pulls her body to his and hugs her tight. Looking over his shoulder she saw one of the boys in the hoodie that she knew, coming towards them.

"Oh hey Luke, I missed you." Tyrone turns around to see who she's talking to, "What da!" Luke has a gun pressed against Tyrone's forehead. Luke smiles deviously, "Gotcha!" He pulls the trigger shooting Tyrone in the forehead.

The bullet goes straight through to the back of his' head splattering blood on Candy's face; she screams! Hearing the gun shot in the hospital caused the people standing nearby to scream and run away. . Tyrone falls to the floor dead and Candy falls to her knees beside him with her forehead to his chest, crying and shouting, "NOOOOOOO! WHY DID YOU HAVE TO DO IT TYRONE?"

The alarm clock goes off and Tyrone wakes up in a panic thinking he was really shot. He jumps up out of his dream sweating and yelling. "AHHHH!

He realizing it was just a dream, he sits on the side of his bed with his hands on his forehead thinking about his nightmare. He rubs his forehead checking his hand for blood. Feeling a little discombobulated, "what the fu#k was that?"

Terrified by the dream, he walks to the bathroom, holding his head as he calms down. Looking at the mirror in his bathroom, he can see sweat on his forehead. He turns on the sink and splashes water on his face. He grabs the hand towel and washes the water from his face as he makes his way to the shower door; sliding the shower door back he turns the water on.

Thinking about his dream, he goes into the kitchen and checks it out making sure he was really alone. Shaking his head smiling to himself, he starts walking down the hall back towards his bedroom. Half way to his room, he hears a hard knock on his front door. Immediately he assumes its Mike. He walks towards the door laughing preparing to tell mike about his crazy dream.

Walking to the door excited "Yo Mike! Why da fu#k you beatin on my door like the Po Po cuz? He quickly opens the door to greet him, but this time it wasn't Mike. "Naw cuz; Not Mike- "Luke!"

Seattle, Washington

The Date with the Devil Continues

Professor Mirado and Racheal head to his Library. As they approach, he pulls in front, telling her to remain in the car, while he checks the security alarms making sure they're off. While Racheal waits in the car, Professor Mirado goes in to speak with the person in charge.

Professor Mirado approaches the front desk, "good evening, lovely day isn't it?" The Librarian smiles, "yes it is, can I help you with something? "Why yes you can, you can point me in the direction of the man in charge, if that may be possible."

The Librarian smiles proudly, "that would be me, is there something I can assist you with?" Professor Mirado smiles, but of course! He taps his finger twice on the desk, and the Librarian becomes a statue. I'm sure you won't mind taking a break now would you? He taps his finger again, and all of the pictures on the walls became portraits of him. Now, that's quite better; all righty then, time for the main course. He goes back to the car to assist Rachael out of the car and into the Library. Entering the Library she's simply amazed.

Looking around Rachael is astonished, "how long has this been here? "He smiles, "I enjoy what I do, and therefore everyday seems as if it's the first." "I can imagine, she says in amazement." Professor Mirado watches Rachael roam around the library. "Where did you get all of these books?"

"Oh I've accumulated them over the years. It seems like centuries." Remembering what he said to her in the mall, "so where's this author you told me you like so much, what's his name." "Ah, you remembered, well now come let me show you." He says with a devious smile. He walks her to the back of the library and picks a book from the shelf and hands it to her. As she reaches for it, he taps his finger twice on his leg, and the book became the story of her life, utilizing different characters. "What's it about?" "I'm sure you'll find it quite interesting, it's based on a true story."

"And what story is that?" "Well, if you insist, it tells the story of a young girl who had a father who preached in a family church, but had an affair with one of his church members or shall I say a guest, however, after their affair, finds himself to be a father three times over, the last one of course, unexpected.

The story goes on to where he shows himself a friend to his true family, only to discover that his wife wasn't too fond of his relationship with them, and without any authority, she burns him to the ground in the church."

"Oh my God; that's horrible, what kind of wife would do something so horrible just because she didn't like his family?" "A wife who truly needs to be revenged upon and his true family insist on making this a reality. I almost forgot the best part; her daughter willing delivers his true family to the wife by way of her ...new lover."

Frowning she looks into his eyes, "it seems to me like she had it coming, I guess I would've done the same thing if it was me." With a devious smile, "I couldn't agree with you more!" "So who authored this book?" "The Authors name happens to be that of my own, Luther." "You've never told me your name before now." He taps his finger against his leg. "Why of course I have, don't you remember?" suddenly remembering, "Oh yeah, I'm sorry, I remember now you did tell me", she says feeling a little strange.

She looks at the book wanting to know more, "can I check this book out, I would really like to find out more about it." Knowing that the book will return to its original state, "I'm afraid not, this is considered a house book, but you're more than welcome to visit it anytime." "Aw," she says playfully frowning; I promise I'll bring it back, just one day."

"Oh, believe me, as much as I would love too, I really couldn't. It's just happens that every book is accounted for electronically and I wouldn't want to mess up the order, or better yet confuse the computer". "Electronically, really I've never heard of anything like that before, how does it work"?

"Well, let me show you", as he walks over to one of the shelves, he removes a book while tapping his leg, and through the intercom speakers you could hear his name spoken in a computerized voice. "Excuse me Mr. Mirado, a book has been removed from the house department." "Wow!, that's so cool, it calls your name and everything. You have so impressed me with everything", she says overly excited.

"Have I, I've only just begun" he says as he softly strokes the side of her face with his hand. "I don't think I can handle any more, if I don't leave not I may never leave; besides, I promised my mother that I would meet her at the house for dinner." "Oh really, how nice". I would indeed enjoy very much the opportunity to meet your mother", he says eagerly. Considering his request, "I would, but I would have to ask her first."

Preparing to tap his leg to change her mind, a costumer walks in and distracts him. He turns his attention to the customer instead. "Excuse me, can you tell me where's Mr. Gordon the Librarian?"

Not wanting Rachael to catch on, he taps his finger attempting to make the customer think he's in the wrong library. "I'm sorry, my dear man, I do believe you have the wrong library, clearly you can see this library belongs to me", as he points to the pictures, and taps his fingers.

This customer is a true man of God and wasn't affected by his taps. No sir, I have been coming to this library for years, I've known him for a long time. "Wait a minute, that's him standing in the corner". "Mr. Gordon are you all right?" The customer's presence over powers Professor Mirado's power, therefore everything began to return back to its normal state. Professor Mirado rushes over to Rachel, who's looking at his pictures on the wall, and notices something different. He quickly grabs her by the hand and taps his finger, but nothing happens.

Curious as of why he grabbed her hand, she inquires, "Is something wrong? Anxious to leave he knew he had depart from the presence of the customer in order for his powers to work on her. "No, not at all, it's just that it's getting quite late I must be getting you back to your car". As he quickly leads her towards the door, she was stops by the customer who realized that he knew her. "Rachael, is that you? Oh My God, look how much you've grown."

Trying to remember, "do I know you?', Smiling as he walks over to her, "it's me Rachael, Carl Thornton, I was the man who used to give you candy every Sunday at your parent's church when you were a little girl, I was the deacon there."

Slowly remembering, "oh yeah, the purple hearts and chocolate bonbons, you used to tell me that the color purple represented royalty and that I had a royal heart." He was happy she remembers him, "that's right, and I still believe that."

Professor Mirado could no longer stand the presence of the Carl's spirit without returning to his true form, he quickly departs from of the building. "I'm sorry if I've held you too long, because I think your friend left you." "Were you two riding together?" Now that he's gone she can't remember anything about him.

"I don't know," She said holding her head; "I remember talking to a man in the mall, who said he was a Professor of some private practice or something. I remember talking to him but I can't remember what we talked about. And then we walking to the garage to see his car or something, but I don't remember anything that happened after that. This might sound crazy, but I don't even remember how I got here."

Carl becomes concerned, "are you ok, do you want me to take you home?" "No, not home, but you can take me to my car at the mall if it's not too much trouble".

"Oh", no trouble at all." He turns to the Librarian Mr. Gordon. "What happened to you"? "Why were you standing in the corner, didn't you hear me asking for you when I came in." Mr. Gordon tries to remember, but draws a blank. "I really don't know, the last thing I remember was talking to a gentleman at my desk, and then I must have blacked out I guess, until you arrived. That's weird, nothing's ever happened to me like that before."

Carl begins to wonder, "I don't know what's going on with you guys, forgetting where you've been or how you got here, but it sounds to me like that man you were with had a lot to do with it."

Rachael curiously responds, "How so?" "I don't know, but it was something about him that just didn't set well with my spirit;" "he must've felt it too, because he got out of here in a hurry. You really have to be careful of who you allow around you, because people are crazy these days. That man could've put witchcraft or something on you two, you just don't know, but whatever it was, it had to leave when the anointing showed up."

Mr. Gordon, Thinking about what Carl said, "you know what, you're sure right, people are crazy, and it seems as though they're getting crazier by the minute. It's almost as if God himself has turned his back on mankind." Carl agrees, "It's definitely time for the world to turn their hearts back to God and pray, because if he has turned his back, that's the only way we can get him to turn back around."

Feeling bad, Rachael confesses, "yeah, I for one know I've slipped away from him in so many ways. I know I need to pray more." Carl puts his hands around her shoulders. "We all have fallen short; it's just time for us to turn back to God in all our ways and deeds. Time is just too short to be out here in a world without the protection of God."

After their conversation, Carl drives Rachael to the mall to get her car. He then follows her home just to make sure she arrives safely. He blows his horn and wave's good-bye as she walks into the house, glad to be home. Entering the house she notices how dark it is. Clicking the light switch on and off, she discovers there's no power. "Mom, what's wrong with the lights".

"Mom are you in here, mom!" Rachael walks towards the kitchen hoping to find some matches, using the light from her cell phone, she searches the kitchen drawers. Finding nothing, she again calls out for her mother, "Mom are you in here, where are the matches, something's wrong with the lights, the power isn't coming on, Mom!"

No answer. She assumes her mother may've stepped out of the house for something. She smells something burning. Rachael makes her way to the oven and opens it. With the light from her phone, she sees a blackened pot roast still sizzling.

Coughing from the smoke, she pulls it out of the oven, throwing it in the sink. Becoming worried, she begins to wonder about the pot roast and why her mother would leave it unattended. Knowing her mother's passion for baking, she realizes something's not right.

Attempting to call her brother Samuel, she can't get a signal on her phone. She decides to go upstairs to see if her mother may have fallen asleep while cooking. As she approaches her mother's room she sees a blazing light beneath the door and a smell of burning wood.

Thinking her mother may be caught in a fire, she turns the knob and rushes in, nearly falling into an enormous hole in the floor with a blazing fire and burning brimstone that consumes her mother's room. Terrified, trying to keep her balance, she reaches back to take hold of the door frame.

Becoming stable, she sees her mother's bed hovering above the open hole. Lying straight in what looks like a trance, with her hands crossed at her stomach. On the right side of her stands Professor Mirado, with a devious, devilish smile reaching for her as if to draw her soul from her body. On the left side of her, stand two tall Angels with drawn swords as if they're ready for battle.

Suddenly Professor Mirado changes into his true form of the Devil. "Ah, Rachael, I've been waiting for you, I knew how much you wanted to know the ending of the book you so anxiously had to see.

"Well now," Here it tis" As he points his sharp index finger at her mother's heart and twirls it in the air as if to wrap her spirit around his finger, he slowly pulls at her soul. As her mother's faith weakens the Angels began to fade.

He laughs with a diabolical laugh, "do come in, the party has just begun!" He taps his finger against is fiery leg and Racheal instantly appears in his arms, horrified, screaming and fighting to get away!

Hollywood, California

Tyler goes to the warehouse to execute his plan. Arriving there, he parks his car in front of the warehouse and walks to the back of the building towards the room Susan's in. arriving at the door of the brick room; he puts his ear to the door and listens for movement. Hearing nothing, he quickly thinks of a plan in case she sees him. Thinking that he would appear as the one who found her, he unlocks the door and opens it.

Slowly he walks into the cold and dark room, a dim light from a broken window on the ceiling is vaguely shinning on her, he can barely see her lying on the floor, and he assumed she's asleep. Kneeling beside her, he gently places his hand on her arm and shakes her. He realizes that her body is cold and tries to move her toward him, but rigor mortis has already set in.

He quickly pulls back, falling on the floor and with his legs scoots back to the wall in the room. Tyler yells, "No! No!-No, this can't be happening, what have I done! What am I going to do?" Suddenly he remembers Sherri in the back seat of his car. Quickly dashing to his feet, he runs out of the room tripping on slabs of concrete. In a panic he rushes through the warehouse to his car, only to discover that Sherri is gone.

In a confused state of mind, Tyler runs around the area yelling for her, "Sherri, where are you, Sherri I'm sorry baby, let me take you to the doctor, Sherri, come on Sherri don't do this to me, d#&%it! Where the hell are you! Sherri! SHER...RI!"

With everything seeming to be spinning around him, he falls against his car crying in a panic. Sliding down the side of the car hitting the ground, he sits there with his hands to his head feeling as if he's losing his mind. "SHER.....RI!" He realizes that the worst is yet to come!

New Hope, Virginia

Grandma Ames and the crew are in route to Seattle, Washington to battle with Karen. Grandma Ames, becoming troubled in her spirit asks, "How much further do we have to go, because I just got a feeling that "just in time" may be too late." Pastor is driving says, "I think we'll be there well before just in time". We're only 45 minutes away from Seattle. Do you have any idea where we're going in Seattle?"

"The Lord keeps showing me the numbers "57394: in my spirits she replies, I'm assuming that must be her address." Yolanda searches for answers, "you said 'her' do you know this woman?" "No, but I feel like I do. This woman whoever she is, her spirit has been pulling at mine. It's as if I can sense her fear of whatever it is that she's facing. I don't know what we're going up against, but whatever it is it has to be powerful, because God has placed so much in me",

Yolanda curiously continues, "So much like what exactly? "Grandma Ames wonders if she should tell them, "well, it started with my eyes, he let me see things all around the world. Then it was my ears, I could hear souls crying for help, living souls, ones who are now looking for peace.

But now, it's my mouth, whatever I say comes to pass, not like normal praying, but I mean really come to pass, I didn't wanna tell y'all this yet, but I guess no time is better than now. I can call upon ten thousand angels and

God has instructed them to obey my call", she explains.

They all look at each other, trembling in their spirits. Realizing this journey in which God has equipped them for, was not just a spiritual battle, but a supernatural war. A war that not only affects mankind, but one that will inevitably erupt the revelations of HELL!

Atlanta, Georgia

Three months after Tammy's admission in the Institution, the doctors realize that her mental condition remained the same. Losing her reason to live, she lays around her room looking at the walls. Due to her lack of appetite, the institution workers were ordered to force feed her.

The Nurse enters Tammy's room, good morning Ms. Johnson, rise and shine; it's time for your breakfast. Tammy doesn't respond. She walks over to Tammy and rubs her on the back of her head.

"Come on Ms. Johnson, we're going to do better with our eating today aren't we? Ms. Johnson are you still with me?" Helping her over to the feeding table, "come on sweetie, it's time to eat now, we don't want you passing out from starvation", Tammy looks her in her eyes as if she wants to say something, uh...uh..., She looks at Tammy concerned, "what is it Ms. Johnson, what are you trying to tell me?"

With tears in her eyes, Tammy struggles to speak, uhhh-I-h-hh-ma-hh-iss-hh-my hhh-ba-baby! She begins to cry. The nurse gently pulls Tammy's head against her side, rubbing her shoulders. "Aw baby, I know...aw honey...it's going to be ok. Just know that your daughter would've wanted you to live and tell the world about your beautiful times together. She wouldn't want you to be in here giving up on life. You have to eat and get better. That's the only way you'll be able to leave this place."

For the first time in three months Tammy begins eating on her own. The nurse is so excited that she rushes out of the room to inform the doctor of the good news. Thirty minutes later the doctor enters Tammy's room in excitement, "well now Ms. Johnson, I've just received the most exciting news of all times, you're now eating on your own, that's wonderful! Let me take a quick look at you" The doctor leans down in front of her with a little flash light and checks her pupils.

"Now that's what I call progress, your pupils are looking good and your cheeks are showing some color now. I think we're on our way to recovery." Tammy speaks in a whisper, "I want to go home!"

"Well, if you keep progressing as you are, you'll be home sooner than later". Tammy's brother, Robert was scheduled to visit with her, as he does every chance he gets. While the doctor's still with Tammy, Robert walked in. "Knock, Knock, how's my baby sis doing today", Robert smiles.

The doctor says proudly, "funny you should ask, it just so happens that she's coming along quite impressively. This morning she started eating on her own, her eyes are looking good, and she just told me that she wants to go home. I'll say your little sis is doing just fine."

Overjoyed, "that's my little sis; I knew you could do it." Walking over to hug her, "come here girl, I am so proud of you. You keep this up and you will be ready to move into my new house I just bought here in Georgia", Tammy smiles, talking in a whisper, "really Robert, you did? I want to go home with you; I don't want to be here anymore."

Robert sits beside her with his arms around her and her head on his shoulder, "you keep improving the way you are and you will" as he kisses her on the forehead. "I spoke with Lieutenant Larson yesterday, and he told me that all of your charges have been dropped, due to temporary insanity.

He said the judge wanted to keep you here for one year, but he talked him into letting you leave on the decision of the institute's director, which means, you have to get better so you can come home, with me." Didn't I tell you that I was going to take care of everything? I love you Tammy, we're going to get through this together, I got you girl, I got you."

Tammy smiles, with tears in her eyes, "I love you so much Robert, I don't know what I would do without you. I'm so sorry for putting you through... "Tammy, you don't have to apologize for nothing, you had every right to feel the way you felt. That was your baby, your only child, my only niece.

What you did is what any mother who loves her child would have done, so don't you ever let me hear you apologize about anything ever again. I love you and I am going to make d$#n sure that nothing or nobody will hurt you ever again." Robert kisses her on the head and hugs her tight. Tammy cries in his arms.

Doctor enters the room, "Mr. Johnson, I don't mean to interrupt your visit, but before you leave, can I see you for a moment, I just need you to fill out some forms for your sister." "Of course, I'll be right in as soon as I'm done here", says Robert. "There's no rush, take all the time you need."

 Robert smiles, "thank you Doctor." Tammy asks, "what kind of forms, I thought we gave them everything they needed." Robert says, "Tammy baby, don't you realize how important you are, your story hit the national news, they will never stop filling out forms about you." They both start to laugh.

Lying on his shoulder, Tammy says in a whisper, "you are so crazy Robert. He laughs, "crazy about you, and don't you forget that. Tammy asks, "Robert how is Kiekie, is she ok?"

Laughing, Robert says, "Well, other than a big fine and a few nights in jail, she's fine. Smashing through that guard rail of a state building while the cameras are rolling wasn't exactly the smartest thing she could've done. I saw that girl yesterday at the gas station; she's just as crazy as ever, she told me to tell you that she's coming to see you soon. I don't know if I want you two to be together again, it's no telling what my Bonnie and Clyde will come up with next." As Tammy, laughs in a whisper, she says, "Robert, you're wrong for that."

Still laughing, Robert says with a smile, "you know I'm telling the truth, that's why you're laughing. I'm going to place some hidden microphones in your room, so that when she gets here I can listen in on your next plot." Tammy is laughing almost in a normal voice. Tammy laughs so hard she has tears in her eyes.

Robert enjoys seeing his sister laugh again, "Girl let me go before the Doctor thinks I'm making you cry and tries to put me out." Hugging her tight, he tells her, "It's good to hear you laugh again Tammy." Kissing her on the forehead, "I love you girl, I need you to get better, so that I can get you out of here. Don't focus on the bad things, think about the good times you had with Rhonda, the way she laughs and the things you two did together. Those are the things I think about, I can deal with it better that way. If you need anything, I mean anything at all, you call me, and I'll be right there for you ok."

They hug each other tight, "I will. I hate it when you leave, I want to go with you so bad", Tammy says. Robert smiles, "and you will, as soon as you're completely better. I love you sis, I'll see you next week, same time same place. You take care of yourself; I need you to get better."

"I will, I promise. I love you too", Tammy says. He kisses her on her cheek and walks out of the door. With tears in her eyes, hating to see him leave, Tammy grabs the guard rail of her bed and pulls herself to her feet. Forcing her legs to move she takes her first step towards the bathroom. Tammy hasn't walked on her own, since she was admitted to the institution. Proud of herself, she takes another step. Making it to the bathroom door, she's interrupted by a voice calling her name.

"Hello Tammy!" Tammy turns to see who it is, in a shock she responds, REGINA! They both stand there looking at each other.

This series continues in volume

2